Grit and GRIND

KAT ADDAMS

ISBN-13: 978-1-7331523-0-3

ONE

Klara's alarm buzzed at exactly 5:07 a.m. every morning. In the past, she'd set it for 5 a.m., but last summer, she'd read an article that changed her waking habits. It was from a study in one of those science magazines that sat, collecting dust, in the dentist's waiting room. Some super-smart panel of super-smart people had conducted an experiment that showed the difference in getting just a few extra minutes of sleep each night. The research concluded that getting as little as seven extra minutes of sleep could be a person's saving grace when that mid-afternoon lull kicked in right after lunchtime. Klara had taken the article's advice and tried it for nearly two weeks before declaring it bullshit. However, the habit stuck, and her alarm continued to go off at 5:07 a.m. every morning. And, without fail, she'd just as quickly hit the snooze button. Twice. Never less, never more.

When her alarm buzzed for the last time, Klara narrowed her eyes and stared at her phone, as if daring it to keep going. At twenty-six, she was still young enough to easily hop out of bed, but she didn't always want to.

She spent too many late nights staring at a blank computer screen with her feet propped up on her desk and nibbling one of those bland "guilt-free" snacks. Her thoughts not on the novel in front of her, but on writing the company who had marketed this glorified chunk of iceberg as some new innovative zero-calorie ice cream. And thus down the rabbit hole she would fall. Klara would go from reading ice cream reviews to clicking a link for funny cat videos. From there, she would follow a link to celebrity gossip, local news, and then finally end up on an online shopping spree.

She had a habit of filling up her cart with all the things she wanted and never, ever checking out. Before she knew it, her evening was gone. It was after midnight, and she still had a blank page in front of her. The blinking cursor not so patiently tapping, waiting on her to move it along.

Lazily, she propped herself up and rolled the hair tie from her wrist, securing her long, tangled curls in a messy bun atop her head. Still dazed and confused from her deep sleep, she sat on the side of the bed, rubbing her eyes the way her mother had told her not to unless she wanted to get crow's-feet. Her mother was full of the good ole Southern gospel. When Klara had finally moved into her own place, her mother had told her, if she kept a dirty house, the men she dated might think she had a dirty twat, too. She thought of those pearls of wisdom while she made her bed. She wondered if any of her past lovers had noticed the thin layer of dust on her picture frames and become confused when they found out she had a perfectly manicured playground.

Klara hurriedly tidied up her sheets and pillows. She couldn't afford to be late to her first writers workshop. Finals were over, and she had been one of the first students to eagerly sign up for the summer writing series. The workshop was being led by Christopher Kaiser. *The* Christopher Kaiser. She had been devouring Christopher's books since she first discovered them her freshman year. He was a well-known Southern writer who specialized in historical fiction with a touch of erotica. She hadn't known she liked history until she picked up one of his books, and it ended up on the floor beside her bed. Right next to her vibrator. From then on, she'd had a sudden interest in historical fiction.

Klara stumbled to the coffeemaker and quickly put on her running gear. She had just enough time to gulp down a cup of cheap, bitter coffee before she headed out the door and toward the river. If she timed it right, she might bump into the hot guy who worked making pasta at the farmers market on Saturdays. She had seen him running in the park at this time the last few days. His dirty-blond hair, tousled from the wind, hanging into his eyes. Sweat beading down his smooth chest and pooling at his shorts line. She didn't know his name, but he looked like a John. Farmer John, she'd decided to call him. He looked like the marrying type. All warm smiles and good deeds. She hadn't had much experience with that in her love life. All of her Farmer Johns had turned out to be Farmer Douche Bags.

"They ain't gonna buy the cow if you keep givin' 'em the milk for free."

Klara's mother's voice echoed in her thoughts.

She was always overprotective of Klara. Especially once Klara's dad had left for a pack of cigarettes and a Michelob and never come back. No calls, no letters, nothing. He just disappeared and for the better, according to her mom.

Klara shook her head as if to get her mom and ghost dad out and let Farmer John back in. She closed her eyes as she thought about what it must feel like to slowly run her hands along a tight body like that. It had been over a year since she even touched another man. Not counting that one-night stand with that guy, Miles, from the bookstore. That had been a complete disaster. She always fantasized about meeting someone at a bookstore. She thought only the interesting, smart guys would hang around there. But, yet again, she had been wrong. She still had no idea how Miles had talked her into bed. It definitely wasn't the man bun ... or the Clark Kent glasses. She shuddered as she tried to forget that night. Miles could not go miles. The only thing that ran miles with Miles was his ego.

She sighed heavily, stepping outside and into the sultry morning air. Today was going to be hot and nasty. She could feel the gritty heat of the Memphis summer already, and the sun hadn't even risen. Klara glanced again at her watch. She was going to have to make this quick. As she headed toward the river, she could see smoke billowing up into the sky. The scent of roasting meat hung heavy in the air around her. The barbeque championship festival was up and roaring downtown. Cars lined every street within a five-mile radius to cross the river, so revelers could party all day and night on Mud Island. Laughter and music drifted across the banks as Klara tucked her headphones in her ears and started her morning run.

At six fifteen a.m., her phone buzzed again to let her know it was time to head back. Exhausted, she sat on the river landing to watch the sunrise and catch her breath. The park was starting to fill with other runners, yoga moms, bodyweight beasts, and the occasional panhandler. She always carried a few dollars tucked in her shorts for those she thought needed it most. One man in particular she was quite fond of helping out. His name was Steve, and he was a veteran. The war had left him permanently brain damaged, and no one would hire him or give him a chance. He was too much of a risk. That was when he picked up the bottle, and the rest was history. At least, that was the story he'd told her the first time he asked for money for booze. She liked his honesty and gave him a twenty-dollar bill. Shocked, he'd graciously bowed down to her and hurried off to the store.

Now, anytime she ran by him, he always shouted, "You're the Memphis queen!"

She always laughed and circled around to give him a few dollars. He probably called all the girls Memphis queen.

Steve wasn't anywhere in sight today, but Farmer John was heading her way and fast. His attention was on the barges churning their way up river, not in front of him where she sat on the edge of the walk. If he didn't look up, he was going to brush right by her, possibly tumble into her. She side-eyed him as he edged closer and closer toward her. Thinking quickly—but very, very stupidly—in the heat of the moment, Klara stood up. With her eyes pretending to watch the sunrise, she took a step backward. Right into the line of fire. Before she could think—because her brain had clearly been zapped by an oncoming six-pack—two hands grabbed her from behind and pulled her away. Farmer John looked up, startled, just nearly missing Klara. He stumbled on his own feet and hit the ground in front of her.

"Are you all right?" he said, looking up at her and the man standing in her shadow.

"Yeah, I think so," she said, slowly turning to look at the person who'd ruined her scheme of building a magnificent life with Farmer John after he tripped, landed on top of her, and fell madly in love with her. She could already see their two twin boys fading in the distance.

The intruder spoke up, "I'm really sorry. I saw you standing there, and neither of you were paying attention! You were off in la-la land, running toward her like a freight train, and she was distracted by your swaying cargo! I was just trying to prevent the train wreck."

Klara looked at the man, shocked. Her mouth hung open, her face flushed with embarrassment and rage, all at once. How dare he call her out like that! And right in front of her future husband!

Farmer John looked visibly uncomfortable, too. He gave a passive laugh and was off and running again before she could apologize. He called over his shoulder that he was sorry and would pay more attention next time, but Klara didn't hear it. She was ready to give Mr. Know-It-All an earful.

"I was *not* checking out his swaying cargo!"

"Yes, you were."

"Um, no ... I wasn't! I was trying to catch my breath from my run, and I was a bit dazed!"

"Yes, dazed by his abs. I must admit, they're really nice abs. Do you think he'd share his secret?"

Klara pursed her lips, noticing for the first time the sexy grin on this man standing before her. She tried to look mad, but she couldn't help herself. She laughed.

"Kale chips, cauliflower rice, açai smoothies, and iceberg ice cream, I'm sure."

"That sounds terrible! What exactly does an iceberg taste like?"

"Watery spit and dashed dreams."

The man peered down at her. He was at least six inches taller than she was, even when she was puffed up and had her feathers ruffled. His scruffy, unshaved face twitched as he tried to figure her out. An awkward silence hung in the air as she guessed she had gone too far with her sarcastic sense of humor. But, to Klara's surprise, he laughed.

"That is damn brilliant! I'm Chris, by the way," he said as he stuck out his hand.

"Nice to meet you, Chris. I'm Klara. And thank you for ... saving me."

"For saving you from a hopeless-romantic love affair had he crashed into you?"

Klara blushed. "I don't know what you're talking about, but I didn't need saving. I was completely aware he was coming too close. I was just slow from my workout. Not distracted," she said, realizing her defensiveness was obvious. She quickly changed the subject. "What exactly were *you* doing, watching *me*, anyway?"

"I was observing you actually," he said as he noticed her tense up. "I mean, not just you. I wasn't observing just you. Damn, I realize this is coming out kind of creepy."

"Mmhmm ... "

"Look," he continued, "part of my work is research, and this just so happens to be where my next project is based. I want to get a feel of the city and its people before I have to do the daily grind."

She cautiously stared at him while he spoke, losing her train of thought in his smile. He didn't look like a creeper. Maybe he really was working, or maybe he was a serial killer. Her next and last bad decision. She started to ask more about his work, but her alarm buzzed and rudely interrupted her questioning. She glanced down at her phone. *Crap!* She was going to be late unless she ran fast all the way back to her apartment.

"Well, I'm usually around at this hour for my run, if I can help you with any questions you have about the city. As a way of saying thanks for your chivalry, of course. I've got to run though. Thanks again!" she called as she jogged up the stairs. She could feel his eyes on her back.

"I'm sure I'll see you around!"

Klara hurried home and jumped in the shower. The water was cool on her flushed skin. Her eyes closed as she tucked herself under the showerhead and let the water run down her face. Her hands glided along her body, and she noticed the tightness in her core. She smiled, impressed with herself. She thought about Farmer John and what it would be like to peer over his shoulders while he crawled on top of her. Oh, how she would love to wrap her legs around that chiseled back and hang on for dear life.

She reached up to turn the knob on hotter, filling the shower with steam. Klara unhooked the showerhead and let it pulsate between her legs. Moaning, she tossed her head back and rested on the cool tiles. She could see his smile as he thrust inside her harder and harder. Farmer John was now working up a sweat and starting to let out grunts as he reached his climax. She imagined herself smiling back at him, encouraging him—except, this time, it wasn't him looking back at her. It was Chris grinning down at her, looking straight into her eyes as he gave that final deep thrust inside her. She gripped the showerhead tighter as her knees began to tremble. Waves of pleasure shook her whole body as she cried out.

Exhausted and out of breath, Klara slid down the wall. She could feel her heartbeat throbbing in her chest, matching the throbbing between her legs. She did not have time for that.

Where did that come from? she wondered.

She sat on the floor of the shower, trying to think of Farmer John but only saw Chris's face. *Why am I thinking of him?*

He had saved her from getting hurt, but he'd also embarrassed her and made her look like a fool. She hadn't known whether to slap him or thank him.

Klara grabbed a towel and dried herself off. She was probably being too hard on him. She often wondered if having too high expectations was a flaw of hers. There was something wrong with every single man she dated, but then again, maybe there was just something wrong with her. She thought she was a good catch, but she was the one having issues with settling down, not any of her exes or her friends. Mostly, she was content to stay home alone with an order of hot wings and Netflix. Some nights, especially during the bleak winters, she did get lonely.

But, even with her ex-boyfriends, nothing had set her on fire or been worth keeping. Brad had sold used cars, and because of this, he smelled like a cheap Christmas tree air freshener hung on a 1970 pimp Cadillac. The stench stuck in her nose, no matter what cologne she'd bought for him. When she started getting nauseated as soon as he came over, it was done. It didn't help matters that he thought he was hilarious, but his sense of humor was cheesy car salesman. The type that made you cringe and feel embarrassed for him.

"I've got a *dil* for you!" he'd once said as he pulled out her dildo from the nightstand.

No … just no.

David had been fun, but she'd lost her attraction to him early on when his hair started migrating from his head to his back. She still stayed because he was a nice guy and treated her well, but she wasn't crazy about him. He was bland, boring, and they only had the predictable vanilla sex on Saturday nights. Missionary, of course. He kept up this charade of being a bore until he forgot to close his browser window on his laptop he'd left open … in his bathroom. Klara thought it was odd he would use a laptop in there, so she glanced at his open tabs.

"What the hell is … oh my God!"

She had never left somewhere so fast in her life. He knew he was busted because he never attempted to call her after she left. He didn't even ask her for his things back from her apartment. She hoped to never have to look into his face again. As soon as she got home, she slipped on a pair of disposable latex gloves, packed his few things up, put it all in a trash bag, and threw it out. She also sanitized her entire place. Klara had declared herself done with dating for a while after that. She didn't have the time to enter the dating world these days anyway. She had to write and keep her head focused on her work.

Klara had wanted to write since she could remember, but between her part-time job and the MFA program, she had been too busy. She found little downtime to write for pleasure and not for homework. Her professors' writing assignments were never very interesting, and the more she typed on and on about boring details in small Southern towns, the more uninspired she became. She wanted to write about things out of the ordinary. Something shocking, toe-curling, spine-tingling, and all those other adjectives littered on the e-published Amazon blurbs. But also, something serious.

Klara wanted her novel to be one of those stories that readers couldn't get out of their heads until long after they finished reading. But something was holding her back, and she wasn't sure what that was. *What the hell am I afraid of? Lack of experience? Fear of commitment?* She rolled these musings around in her head, realizing that her writing issues were beginning to sound like her dating issues. She tucked that thought into the back of her brain and made a mental note to schedule therapy sometime in the near future.

Klara checked the time on her phone again. If she wasn't out the door in thirty minutes, she would be late for sure. She quickly raided her closet for something mature but still very much bright-eyed and bushy-tailed. She settled on linen shorts and a floral top. Her closet was full of floral prints. Klara had always been drawn to flowers. Roses in particular. Her parents owned a flower farm, and so she had always been surrounded by them. Her green thumb had helped her land her part-time job at the florist. She ran the outreach program, planting flowers in low-income neighborhoods. Her team also worked with the residents on building and cultivating their own gardens.

Klara loved her time with visiting these neighborhoods. It was her little escape. Working with her hands in the soil and her headphones in her ears, she forgot the world around her. Her assignments went poof, her novel went poof, Miles went poof. She enjoyed getting to know the residents despite the fact that most of them were older and cranky. One resident, Ms. May, always made Klara smile even though she had the sassiest mouth on her. Ms. May wasn't afraid to tell Klara if the azaleas she'd planted looked like shit. She also wasn't afraid to ask all about Klara's personal life. Why wasn't she married? Why didn't she have babies? What was she waiting for? She let Klara know that her biological clock was ticking every time she saw her, but that didn't bother Klara. She was close to Ms. May. They had an odd love-hate relationship.

Klara took a quick detour to check on Ms. May's flowerbeds. It would only take an extra few minutes, and she needed to make sure her project wasn't dying in this heat. She parked her car in front of Ms. May's house and walked up the stairs to the porch. The door quickly swung open.

"Hey there, flower girl! You mean to tell me you still ain't knocked up yet? You know I have four grandbabies already from my daughter, and she's about the same age as you. What's wrong with you?"

"Ms. May! I'm not even married yet!"

"That's why I'm askin', what's wrong with you?"

"I guess I'm just too good-looking. They can't handle all this." Klara acted innocent in her sass as she deadheaded the petunias.

Ms. May sucked in her breath and shook her head, trying not to laugh. "How old are you, darlin'? Men don't wait forever. You'd better go out there and find him before he finds somebody else. The only ones gonna be left are gonna be packin' baggage or gonna be packin' something else if you know what I mean. They gonna like Kens, not Klaras."

Klara laughed loud enough to echo through the front porch. She thought dating must have been easier back when Ms. May was young. When women didn't have to worry about much more than finding a husband.

"Is that so?" Klara teased with her hands on her hips. "And you and Mr. May are happily ever after, if I may ask?"

She already knew he wasn't in the picture. Ms. May had told Klara her life story several times before. She just knew she had to be sassy back to Ms. May because that was how she got the old lady to communicate.

"Lawd, child, no! You may not ask! But I'm gonna tell you anyway. I got rid of his old crusty butt years ago. I got my babies, and that's all I need."

Klara shook her head. Ms. May always made her day.

"That's something! They still put up with you? You must make a mean Sunday supper," Klara said, watching Ms. May faintly put her hand to her heart as she pretended to be taken aback. "I'll be back next week to check on these. Be sure to water them daily, so they don't shrivel up like you!"

Ms. May laughed loudly at that. She was a tough nut to crack, but banter seemed to be the only way to her heart.

"Child … child … what am I gonna do with you? Clock's tickin', baby. Your flower gonna shrivel up, too … and fall off if you don't use it!"

Klara loved that old lady. She glanced down at her clock again. Ms. May was right; it was ticking. She had fifteen minutes to get on campus and have her butt in the seat. She pushed the gas pedal down and quickly made her way to school. She had never met a published author before, much less one who was so successful. Klara had been lucky to get into the workshop when she did. It had sold out within hours after it was posted.

She was excited to have the opportunity to pick Christopher Kaiser's brain. Perhaps he could help her get where she needed to go. But that was the problem; she didn't even know where her stories needed to go. She kept drawing a blank, uninspired and too stuck in her head to let herself in anyone else's. She thought she knew what she wanted, but she was stumped on how to get there. It was so frustrating to be on the edge and not able to just spill over. She knew writers who had said they would suddenly have an idea and sit and write for hours and hours. They would forget the time and not even stop to eat. That never happened to Klara.

As she pulled into the parking lot, she wondered what kind of life Christopher must have to write about such erotic experiences. He must be a dirty old man. Who else wrote basically porno history? Old, sex-deprived men—that was who. Or maybe his wife actually was his inspiration in that department. Maybe they had wild, crazy sex in the old mansions and gardens he toured. Maybe she was his muse. Klara thought about that and how it must feel to have a husband whisper filthy things in her ear. How it must feel to be the object of someone's desires. How, even after being married for so long and growing old, that spark for each other never died.

No way. He's totally just a dirty old man.

Klara checked herself in the rearview mirror, grabbed her bag and laptop, and headed toward the classroom. She glanced at the time on her phone—8:44 a.m. Right on time. She yawned as she climbed the stairs, suddenly feeling the exhaustion from her early morning run. It wasn't even lunch yet, and those seven extra minutes of sleep were proving her theory that the study was complete bullshit.

She looked around the hall, searching for the right classroom. She didn't want to sit in the wrong classroom like she had that one time her sophomore year. She realized about two minutes in that she was not in Children's Fiction, but instead, she was in Mandarin. She had been too humiliated to get up and make a walk of shame, so she'd sat and learned the Mandarin symbol for bean. It was cute, like a flowerpot.

She double-checked her schedule—room 342. Klara was in the right place. The room was quiet and empty. She flicked on the lights and made her way to a desk in one of the middle rows, close to a window. As if she needed any distractions. She tucked herself away so as not to appear too fangirl on the first day. She was just settling in and opening her laptop when she heard him.

"Perfecting that romance novel, I suppose? The one where you crash into Mr. Abs at the park, and you both run off into the sunset?"

Klara looked up, temperature rising. Chris from the park. Chris who had saved her. Chris with the sarcastic smirks and know-it-all attitude. Chris … topher. Christopher Kaiser.

TWO

Chris woke early to the city lights still flickering through his window. He lay awake in bed, trying to figure out why he was up before sunrise. He didn't have to teach until nine, which was still too early for him. He preferred sleeping until mid-morning, as he usually spent all night writing, editing, and preparing for his classes. His best work came from the midnight hours, when everything and everyone around him shut down. Silence, peace, no distractions.

Back home, on Captiva, it became quiet and calm after ten p.m. The lazy island life had spoiled him. Memphis was different. He had been kept up all evening by the laughter and cheers from outside his hotel. The service desk at The Peabody had warned him that he would be booking during a very busy weekend of festivals. But Chris didn't mind. Chris wanted to experience all Memphis had to offer. He hoped to soak it up and funnel it into his next masterpiece.

From the moment he'd heard about the history of Memphis, he knew he had to investigate. The books he read had advertised it as a cutthroat river town. Scandals had always riddled the city, then and now. The city was rich in brothels, saloons, corruption, murder, mayhem. The things that made his readers hungry for more. Something wicked yet sexy. He didn't have a clue what he would write about yet, but he figured, with a little bit of research and digging, something would present itself. Something or someone needed a story told. That was how it always happened. He let his imagination take him wherever it wanted to go. His research led him around ancient cemeteries, old and dilapidated buildings, long-forgotten parks, and cold, sterile museums. If he was fortunate, his wanderings led him right to a local heroine of his own.

His muses, he called them. There was Nicole, the curator from Charleston. Her laugh was like that of a choking beaver, but she'd devoured him in the hotel room and been eager to help fuel his erotica during his short stay. Lexi in Richmond, not his usual type, personality-wise. She had been obnoxiously loud and could do an impressive keg stand. But again, she'd kept his brain alight in the bedroom when he struggled with dirty details in that particular novel. Sarah from New Orleans had proven that fat-bottom girls really did make the rockin' world go round. And, lastly, there was Cary. Cary had known the California coastline like the back of her hand. She was a bit older than Chris and much more experienced. The erotica he had written about in his latest novels, all personal experiences with her. She was a gold mine of history and lust.

Chris was lucky. His job gave him the opportunity to experience many different cities, cultures, and women. He was the envy of his male friends back home, who always asked him to elaborate on his escapades. They needed to live vicariously through him, thinking Chris's bachelor life was every man's fantasy. They longed to put themselves in his shoes, but Chris made them work for it. Never one to kiss and tell, he had them read his novels for details. He was, however, open to questions after they finished. Their wives often read his works, too. He knew which ones were fans when their hugs became a little tighter, their laughs at his jokes a little longer. Chris enjoyed the attention. He knew he had a good life, and although his muses kept his mind in erotic mode, he never let that cross over into something more.

He carefully chose the women he let into his life. He knew which ones were capable of not becoming attached and distracting him from his work. Those bawdy, carefree-type of women were also naturally attracted to him, too. They must have sensed his no-strings-attached and no-drama approach. His lifestyle couldn't withstand a relationship anyway—or was it that a relationship couldn't withstand his lifestyle? It wasn't that he didn't want someone to come home to, but that side of his brain he hadn't opened up since his writing career took off. His time and energy had been spent establishing himself in a career he was passionate about. He wasn't concerned with settling down or falling in love.

Writing was his love. He had been writing and traveling since he was twenty-four, and now, he was thirty-six and in a secure and happy place—or at least, he thought he was. His last novel's reviews were less than stellar.

That novel, based on the prostitutes of the Wild West era, was his least popular work to date. He had all of the usual elements that his readers devoured. Sex, suspense, more sex, historical facts, modern-day relations, more sex, tragedy, heartbreak, and more crazy, wild sex. It was, after all, based around prostitutes. He wasn't sure what had gone wrong. However, just barely cracking the best-seller lists jarred him a little. It was as if the ride he was on—this big, fancy pie-in-the-sky hot-air balloon that was his life—was slowly coming back down.

He wondered if this was the end for him. *Is my time to shine over? Have I hit that sweet spot in my career, and this is it? Is it all downhill from here?*

He hadn't had time to figure it all out, as the opportunity to branch out in his career arrived on his doorstep in the form of Marcy.

Marcy was like a big, squishy marshmallow that Chris had known his whole life. She had worked as his father's assistant ever since he was a child. She was his entertainer, caretaker, and teacher during the long hours that Chris had to spend at his father's office. His mother, also flourishing in her own career at the bank, had joked often about how Marcy was her sister-wife or Chris's second mom. He thought, if Marcy didn't have a family of her own, his parents would have seriously considered moving her in with them. She was family and maybe even more so family than his own. Chris's parents had lived busy and fulfilling lives, tied around their careers. It wasn't until two years ago that they decided to retire and enjoy what years they had left.

Now with the family business sold and Marcy out of work, she had begun her own voyage of self-discovery. Much to her grandchildren's dismay, she joined them at college, where she also learned that she loved to write. She was the celebrity of her creative writing classes when word got out that she personally knew a real celebrity—Christopher Kaiser. Of course, she had no idea how that had happened. It wasn't like she'd mentioned his name. Not a lot anyway. Only every other class and a few in between.

"Well, my good friend Christopher Kaiser said ..."

Even though his days were busy with writing, Chris couldn't refuse her when she wanted him to speak on the topic of romance novels in her class. He didn't even hesitate to accept her offer because he owed much of his love of writing to Marcy. She had introduced him to a vast array of books at a very young age and always encouraged him with his schoolwork and creativity. He graciously accepted her request, and in a matter of days, the university had sent him a formal invite and offered him a nice fee. He had taken the plunge down this new career path, and surprisingly, he actually enjoyed it.

After that first seminar, other schools had begun requesting him for more speaking engagements, workshops, classes, and even full-on teaching positions. He quickly dived into the flexible offers, as it allowed him to travel and do his research and write freely. Marcy was only too happy to help him with his bookings, attending events alongside him when she could. He'd hired her on as his part-time assistant when his schedule started to become too overwhelming. With a different city every month already booked out for the next year, he would be lost without her help now.

Chris groggily made his way to the shower, determined to make the most of his time since he was awake early. He remembered a corner coffee shop he'd spotted while checking in the day before and hoped they would be open at this ungodly hour. Though with the amount of traffic in and around town at all hours, he assumed places around here probably never even closed.

He quickly dressed and made his way downstairs. The mezzanine was eerily quiet. His footsteps on the marble floors echoed throughout the halls. *Didn't I read about a haunting here?* Maybe he could work that into his story. He took a moment to take in his surroundings. It was truly a beautiful place. He imagined what it must have looked like about one hundred fifty years ago. *The stories these walls could tell.*

Outside, the air was thick with humidity and the lingering scent of barbecue. He inhaled deeply and groaned in a primal-caveman sort of way. For a split second, he really craved a beer in his hand. He hungrily looked around. This city was already beginning to grow on him. He assumed this divine scent was coming from the festivals across the riverbanks. The smoke curled up and over to him, luring him to make his way to the river and check it out. He dipped into the corner store for a quick cup of coffee and headed down.

The riverfront was slowly waking up as the sun started to rise. The sky changing from purple dusk to cotton candy. Chris sat on a bench, sipping his coffee and looking out over the bluff. He observed the panhandlers, the yoga moms, the cyclers, and the runners.

He tried to imagine why anyone would be up so early. *What dragged these people out of bed at this time? Why would they choose to come here in this hot, sticky mess instead of a cool air-conditioned gym? Is it the endorphin high? Adderall? Do people still use cocaine?*

He couldn't imagine waking up and running around with that much energy. His gym sessions were long after dinnertime, which was usually when he was the most alert.

Chris sat, watching the energetic characters unfold around him. One runner in particular caught his eye. He had seen her running when he first arrived. Her legs moving gracefully up and down the paths. Her face becoming pinker and pinker as she tuned the world out and raced down the river. He saw her fade from view and circle back around. Chris made his way toward the banks to get a closer look.

Oblivious to anyone around her and so deep into the music playing through her headphones, she started singing. Very loudly and very badly. She twirled around and collapsed on the grass right ahead of him. He wondered what she was listening to and what had made her smile like that. He could barely make out any words between her heavy breaths when, suddenly, she stopped, her attention elsewhere. Her eyes were focused in the distance, not moving from her target. She hurriedly put her headphones away.

Chris noticed what, or who, had caught her attention. He looked to be all of six-eight, built like Superman, and was barreling toward her like The Flash. His eyes gazed out at the river, but his muscular legs took him straight ahead. Straight toward the woman. She was biting her lip, but her eyebrows were pinched in what Chris recognized as conflict. She was lusty and calculating. He saw her quickly rise up as the oblivious man came closer and closer.

Don't do it.
Don't do it.
Don't do it.
She's going to do it.

Chris, thinking quickly, sprang into action and made his way down the path. He was going to have to save this silly woman from a concussion. Although it was clear that her brain had already been zapped. He couldn't blame her though; the dude did look like a superhero. Chris looked up to see the man running toward them both as he watched the woman turn her head away and step back into the line of fire. His feet practically skated toward her as he reached out and pulled her back into him for a brief second. Then, he let her go.

He nervously caught his breath and explained to the two confused strangers what had just happened. He mansplained. He didn't know it at the time; he was just happy to have helped. But, as the woman turned to look at him, he was a bit terrified. He could feel the blood draining from his face as her eyes shot through him like darts. He wondered if he could just ask her to go back to singing sweetly, but he got the feeling that would be a very bad idea. He had two choices: he could play up his role as her hero and be astonished that she didn't find him amusing or he could make her laugh. Chris did what came natural to him when he was uncomfortable. He made her laugh. And, to his surprise, she made him laugh, too.

His eyes followed the woman, Klara, as she ran up the stairs and out of sight. Her frazzled curls bouncing as they escaped the granny bun on her head. Granny bun. He didn't think she would like that. Her ... very sexy librarian bun. He wanted to reach over and take the tie out of her hair, letting her curls loose and wild. He pulled his phone out and set his alarm early, so he could stumble into her again the next morning.

As Chris made his way back to the hotel, he noticed people all around him. He could hear music drifting out of several places already. The damp heat started to wear him down as soon as he walked back into his room. He fell back on his bed and stared at the ceiling. His thoughts went back to the city, Superman, Klara, barbecue. Grabbing his laptop, he jotted down details of the sights he had taken in this morning. He decided he would return to the riverbanks at dusk to get a glimpse of the nightlife and compare notes. Flickering neon signs and smoky bars filled his head. The city—dirty, hot, gritty, and rough around the edges.

Finally, he could see his new novel coming together. He wondered if that firecracker from this morning had had anything to do with it. He shook the thought from his head. He had to focus on navigating this city and getting to work.

Lately, Chris had led so many writing workshops that they were starting to all run together. The past few months had been so busy that, sometimes, he wasn't sure which city he needed to be at and when. His novels were taking the backseat to his workshops, and he wasn't yet comfortable with that. He made a mental note to tell Marcy to slow it down. When the workshops had started up, his lifestyle had changed from that of leisure travel and writing to schedules, schedules, and more schedules. Though he was happy with his career opportunities, he was having a hard time adjusting. He didn't want to be like the people he observed around him. Busily rushing from one task to the other. But, today, he had already been knocked off his game. He quickly got ready and headed to the university.

Chris checked his watch before heading into the building. The students should be arriving any moment now. It was a small workshop this time. Only fifteen students allowed. He liked those better, as not only did he get to help the students individually, but he also got to get inside their heads. Usually, that helped him with his own writing. He was well known for his talent in character development. Most of his workshops centered on this skill. Rarely did his ideas come from his imagination, but real-life situations. People-watching and observing all and everything around him. He liked to take a more *stop and smell the flowers* approach to life. So far, it had proven successful. Although, with his head usually in the clouds, he could often get lost in his wanderings. It had its drawbacks, but it was a life that suited him and his career. He couldn't imagine how much his work would suffer if he was firmly on foot, in one place, all the time.

Chris turned the corner toward his classroom; his senses heightened as he followed an intoxicating scent. Honeysuckle? Daisies? Nectar? Something floral, something exotic. He followed his nose down the hall, checking the numbers above the doors—342. He'd arrived. With his head swimming in what smelled like a romp in the garden, he peeked into his classroom. There was only one student inside, but he instantly recognized the curls, the delicate movements, the dreadful but happy humming.

Klara.

The scent of her perfume hung in the air, surrounding Chris.

Floral. Like a rose with thorns.

He stood in shock, unsure of how to approach her. She still hadn't noticed him yet, standing there like a weirdo with his mouth open. He had to think. And quick.

"Perfecting that romance novel I suppose? The one where you crash into Mr. Abs at the park, and you both run off into the sunset?"

Damn it. That was probably the wrong approach with her.

Klara slowly lifted her gaze up to meet him. Her eyes narrowed. He was pretty sure, if looks could kill, he would have suffered a mild heart attack this morning, and she would be finishing the job right now. Chris was enjoying being a tease, and even though her posture looked ready to pounce, he could see a flicker of a smile beneath those lips of hers. He thought she might slightly enjoy being teased, too, except he would guess that she would never admit it. With footsteps echoing through the halls behind him, he turned to greet the other students before she ever got to respond to his unwelcome wit.

The class flowed through the usual process. Introduction, syllabus, goals, and questions. Chris made sure to personally connect with each student, but his gaze kept coming back to Klara.

He checked his class roster for her full name—Klara Woods. *A beautiful name for a beautiful woman.*

He couldn't keep his eyes off of her. Her hazel eyes, her dark, almost-gothic hair. The way she crossed her legs and then uncrossed them. Her chest rising and falling with each breath. She must know he was watching her again. When their eyes met, she smirked and nodded at him as if she knew exactly what he was thinking. He continued the lecture, pacing back and forth. He could see her out of the corner of his eye. Her gaze never left him.

As the students started working quietly on the assignment, he sat at his desk, opened his laptop, and peered out over the class. Klara's eyes were on the paper in front of her, but he could see she was struggling as she quietly tapped the pen on her paper. She was distracted and unable to focus. He wondered what she was thinking about as she looked up and met his eyes again. His stare didn't waver. He locked eyes with her and cocked his head to the side. She blushed and cast her eyes back down to her paper.

Just then, the clock dinged, and the students began shuffling their things into their bags. Chris made his way over to Klara while she packed up.

"Well, you're quite a surprise. I wouldn't have guessed you as the writing type."

"What the heck is that supposed to mean? How exactly does a writing type look?"

"No, I didn't mean that! Shit! I meant ... "

"Would you like a shovel, so you can dig yourself a little deeper in that hole you started this morning?" Klara looked up at him, one hand on her hip.

He was used to Southern women. He could handle her. Couldn't he?

He laughed and shook his head.

"I would guess," she continued, "you aren't the writing type, seeing as you can't find the right words."

"Touché." He grinned. "Tell me about why you're here. What are you really writing about? I'll not pick on you anymore. I'm interested."

Klara bit her lip, thinking. She wasn't even sure how to answer that because she had no idea what she was even writing about. "I don't know actually. I've been struggling a bit. I have a hard time focusing on my characters and feeling out their emotions. I was hoping your class could help with that, but so far, the only emotion I'm getting is an overwhelming need to give you a swift kick in the ass."

"I do deserve that. I think I might have been a little too teasing toward you with my odd sense of humor. Please accept my apologies."

He looked sincere, but Klara wasn't easily tricked with puppy-dog eyes. She gave him the benefit of the doubt and smiled.

"You did good today, by the way. *Not* this morning. Although, technically, yeah, I'll have to admit, you did good there, too. What I mean is, your class was helpful today."

"Thank you. I hope you can get something out of it," he said as she zipped up her bag and headed toward the door.

"Me, too," she said, flashing a smile.

She was halfway down the hall when he called her back.

"Klara, wait! I have a proposition for you. You said you owed me for my chivalry this morning, right? I have my own project I'm working on, based here, in the city. Can you show me around some? Introduce me to the local scene? Maybe we can make a trade-off, and I'll take you on a character observation?"

"Is that like what you were doing to me this morning? Observing my character?"

Chris flushed, thinking if he should admit he was observing her or checking her out. Which one would scare her off more? He decided he would be vague. It wasn't a lie if you just omitted the dirty creeper details, right?

"Yeah, kind of."

"Fine. But don't expect me to be 'saving' anyone," she said as she raised her eyebrows and turned to go.

Air quotes. She'd made air quotes.

Chris cringed, watching her go. He didn't know if he was more turned off or more turned on.

THREE

It was bright and early Saturday morning when Klara pulled up to the hotel lobby. Chris was already waiting and dressed in his Sunday best.

"You do know we'll be getting our hands dirty in the mud today, right?" she said as she looked over Chris's slim-cut jeans, his leather dress shoes, and white button-up top. Several bouquets of flowers were spilling over his arms.

"What? I thought we were interviewing local residents today and bringing them flowers?"

"Not those kinds of flowers." Klara laughed. "We're planting flowers! And, yes, we'll be talking with the neighbors some, too. I work for a charity through a local florist. Our mission is to brighten up the neighborhoods for the elderly and disabled who can't work their yards themselves."

"Oh. Well, crap. Here ya go. Happy Hot Summer's Day," Chris said as he handed her the bouquets.

"No, no. Let's still give them out. I think it's a great idea actually. Just put them in the back."

Klara motioned toward the backseat of her car. She had driven through a carwash and vacuumed it out right before she picked him up, but the smell of lost and forgotten French fries still lingered from somewhere she couldn't reach. The carwash only had those cheesy Christmas trees for air fresheners, so she'd bought a handful of spring fresh scents and shoved them under her seats.

"Wow, I didn't notice how good these flowers smell," he said as he set them down and hopped in the passenger seat.

Klara held her tongue and let him believe it was the flowers and not the six hundred eighty-seven air fresheners hiding in her car. "That's because they're from my store. Good choice," she said, noticing the gold embellished wrapping.

"Save the girl. Bring the flowers. I impress myself sometimes."

"Hold up there, buddy. This isn't one of your romance novels. You'll be getting super sweaty and dirty today, and I'm sorry to say, but your clothes might get ruined."

"You've read my novels, right? I can definitely do sweaty and dirty."

Klara blushed, realizing her instructor was flirting with her. There had to be some law against that. She was going to let him romanticize this outing and see how quickly he learned to hate the sun this time of year. She smiled as she thought of the work he was in for. Mr. Saves The Day was about to be put through the wringer and get a taste of that good ole Memphis grit. Maybe a bit of hard labor would cure his cockiness. But she had to admit, she did find his confidence and go-getter attitude pretty damn hot. Especially after all the Farmer Lazybones and Farmer Douche Bags.

"I think we are talking about a different kind of dirty, but ya never know. There are some awfully lonely elderly women in this neighborhood who would probably jump on the chance to get down and dirty with you."

Chris laughed at the banter. He had to be on his toes and prepared for anything with Klara. She was a firecracker. She wasn't like the rest. Easily meltable.

She bites, he thought.

They pulled up next to the community produce garden. Several people were already working—pulling weeds, harvesting herbs, replanting and moving the crops. Klara quickly introduced Chris to the volunteers and grabbed a cart. They filled it with gardening tools, gloves, flowers, and the bouquets Chris had brought along.

"Ready?" she said as he swiped a bead of sweat off his brow.

He was already cooking in this heat.

"I'm always ready."

"These ladies are going to eat you alive."

"Bring it." He smirked.

Chris and Klara started near the end of their route and worked their way up the street. They stopped at each house, delivering their bouquets and checking the flowerbeds. She showed Chris how to deadhead the flowers and check for signs of disease or rot. Each resident came out to watch and enjoy the company. Many of these women, and a few men, were skeptical at first of Chris and his questions, but they slowly opened up once he explained to them his stories and what he was writing.

Klara smiled at him as he gently took one lady's hand and led her down the porch steps to show her the new blooms on her roses. He listened intently to the men and women who told tales of growing up in a segregated town. She noticed the smiles on the women's faces as he handed off the bouquets. His charisma had been winning everyone over. The way he moved, the way he talked, his ideas, his laughter, his kindness, his brain. He was damn near perfect. She could see herself easily falling for him if she let herself. But she couldn't let herself. He was only here a few weeks, and it would just end up in heartbreak.

She enjoyed the sexual tension, the banter, the flirting. Maybe she would just keep her walls up and let herself have some fun. She should loosen up; she knew it. But with her instructor? She had this secret internal debate, all the while mindlessly digging and planting, pruning and watering. Klara went back and forth in her mind while she did the dirty work. He offered to help, but she knew he was here for his research, and she knew the residents loved the attention anyway. A lot of them never had company. Their kids, all grown and moved out of the city. There were still a few young families in the neighborhood but not on this street. This street, Ms. May had said, was Dusty Row. Mostly left alone and respected, but neglected and forgotten. Just like its elderly residents.

Chris gave his undivided attention to the neighbors and their stories. He loved hearing about real-life struggles and the history of the city. How times had changed and how they hadn't. He sat, listening, halfway fidgeting and guilt-ridden for not being on his knees in the mud beside Klara, but she'd insisted, and her stubbornness was not something he wanted to toy with right now. So, he listened to the narrators and enjoyed the show. His mouth watered as he caught sight of her kneeling in the grass, bending over, hips slightly raised. Her fitted tank showing the slightest glimpse of cleavage while she leaned forward and aggressively dug out a hole and then very gently placed a flower inside.

He watched as her skin warmed in the sun and started to glow with tiny sparkles of sweat. Her hair, frazzled and up again in the sexy librarian … not granny … bun. Once or twice, she had looked up and caught his eye, but just as quickly, she had looked away and kept working. Her entire focus on the task in front of her.

Is her mind elsewhere? He thought he could pick up on a hint of hesitation, backtracking, thinking.

Maybe she was in her element and using her creativity. Maybe this was how she worked, and he was slowly learning that he so loved to watch her work.

Klara stepped back, admiring the flowerbeds, as he admired her. She was covered in mud, dirt, grass, and sweat, and he had never seen someone so beautiful in his life. The neighbor's words ran together and faded. Time had stopped. He needed her then and now. He wanted to grab her and pull her to the side of the house, behind the bushes, and take her against the bricks. His heart beat faster as he imagined his lips on hers, her breath on his neck while her legs wrapped around him. That first moment he entered her, a cry of relief for them both. Her arms holding on as he thrust harder and harder when she cried, *Yes! Yes! Yes!* Their moans stifled as they sneakily gave in to their desires.

"Are you okay? Do you need some water?" the neighbor said as she woke Chris from his trance.

Her husband, sitting beside her, slowly shook his head and grinned. Without saying a word, they both knew what Chris really needed was not water. The man winked and looked the other way. Pretending he didn't see into Chris's dirty mind as he fantasized about the beautiful woman in front of him.

"Water would be great. Thank you!" he barely choked out, tugging at his collar. The sweat now dripping from his brows.

Klara looked over at them all, seemingly not paying attention, but he thought he could see a glimmer of mischief in her eyes.

It was nearing lunchtime when they reached the last few houses, including Ms. May's. Chris had by now unbuttoned his shirt a bit, loosened his collar, and dabbed his hairline with a glove. Klara was impressed by his silent suffering. She couldn't believe he was still hanging in there.

"You might as well just take it off now anyway. I don't know how you are even surviving in jeans! Do you want to skip the rest and leave?"

Chris looked around, defeated. With one swift movement, he pulled his shirt off and over his head. Klara stopped walking and could have sworn that the heavens parted and shone down on him in that moment. Her jaw dropped as she took in his extremely fit physique.

Why, oh why was he hiding that under there? And why, oh why is he doing this to me?

There had to be something terrible about him. Something, anything. He was too good to be true. Maybe she should just ask him to take his pants off, too. She needed an excuse, a fault, something wrong with him so that she wouldn't fall for him. Maybe he was hiding a pickle. A gherkin. Tiny, odd-shaped, leaning too far to the right. Not that it would matter. Much. Motion in the ocean and all. Right?

"Earth to Klara." He laughed. Loving every moment of watching her lose her focus. "I forgot what abs did to you. Tsk, tsk. Shame on me. I'm not sure I can save you from this situation. I'm not really sure I even want to."

"Yeah? So, what's *your* secret? I'll admit, I'm a bit shocked. I think you might be able to give Farmer John a run for his money."

"Farmer who?"

"Nothing." She blushed. She'd forgotten that Chris didn't know she had given the hot guy a silly nickname.

"Wait a minute. Farmer John? Abs … is that the guy at the river? Is that really his name?"

"I don't know his name. But, yes, he's Farmer John to me. I've got a bit of a quirky-nickname habit. Just add it to the list of shames you already know about me."

"So then, what's my nickname?"

"I haven't given you one," Klara lied.

She ran through the list in her head she had been toying with recently. Cocky Chris, Conflict Chris, Chris Stiffer, Gherkin. It had to be a gherkin. He couldn't be blessed in all areas. Her thoughts trailed off as he made his chest muscles dance for her.

They both laughed loud enough that everyone nearby stopped to stare.

"I don't believe that for a minute. Come on, tell me."

"I'll let you know when I think of one. I'm still working on my character development. Remember, you're helping me with that?"

"Okay, okay. I do owe you some help in that area. Character observation was the deal, right?"

"Right."

"But you owe me a nickname after."

"Oh, I'll give you a nickname. You might not like it, but I'll come up with something."

They giggled their way to Ms. May's house, pulling the almost-empty cart behind them.

"Just so you know, the lady who lives here is very special to me. She's about as edgy as they come at this age but in a good way. She always looks out for me even if she doesn't want to admit it."

"Edgy, huh?"

"Edgy is putting it nicely," Klara said.

"They don't grow them like that where I'm from. What's in the water around here anyway? Vodka?"

"Ha! I could use a bit of that water right now."

"Tonight?"

"What?"

"The character observation. Let's get that cocktail, and our debts will be repaid. Just need the nickname, and you'll be free to go."

"But I ... " Klara tried to respond quickly, not knowing what to say. She wanted to pick his brain, but she hadn't known there would be alcohol involved. She could see herself losing to the vodka, his abs, his smile. They kept walking as she stammered, racking her brain for an excuse.

"Lawd, Jesus Almighty, Klara girl. What is it you brought me today?" Ms. May stepped out on her porch, leaned against the doorway, and dramatically fanned herself.

"Well, I brought you roses to replace the ones you don't bother to water, and I also brought you a friend of mine. His name's Chris, and he has some questions. He's writing a story, and he needs more information on the locals. Just about life growing up in the city and any local history you know."

Ms. May still fanned herself as Chris handed her a bouquet.

"Pleased to meet you, Ms. May." Chris stuck out his hand to shake hers.

"The pleasure is mine," she replied, raising her eyebrows. "Klara, honey, can you help me inside before you get started? I'll bring us out some sweet tea."

"Sure," said Klara.

She had only been in Ms. May's house twice before. It was like stepping back into time. The crackled gold mirrored wall at the end of the hall. The parquet flooring, the doilies, the Tiffany lamp above the dining table. The scent of mothballs and stale coffee knocking you over as you entered the door. It was a very much lived-in house. Things falling apart but still grandma clean. Ms. May always took pride in her home. She was forever a homemaker.

"What the hell, Klara? You'd better tell me this is who gonna give you all them babies. Because that is some good genes right there! Why didn't you tell me you had a boyfriend?"

"Well, he's not my boyfriend. He's my instructor at school."

"Oh Lawd! I didn't know you was that nasty," Ms. May said as she gave Klara a little wink.

"It's so not like that, Ms. May! Oh my gosh! I'm helping him; he's helping me. It's all business."

"You need to be up in his business. Look at that."

They both stared out the kitchen window as Chris took a shovel and started digging the old rose bushes up. His chest and shoulders flexing with each movement. The sunlight reflecting off the sheen of sweat he was covered in, making him dazzle in a fiery glow. Both women were breathing heavier as they watched him work. Ms. May started to fan herself again.

"He does look damn delicious, doesn't he?" Klara said. Her voice raspy with desire.

"Is he good? A gentleman? Is he nice to you? Does he cook and clean? I know he has a good job! That's a big deal right there."

Klara laughed at Ms. May's twenty questions. She knew the old lady cared about her.

"Almost too good. Too good to be true. I didn't know you cared this much about me, Ms. May."

"Who said I'm asking for you, honey? Can't Ms. May have some fun, too? I'm old, but I'm not dead."

Ms. May pulled herself away from the window to pour a few glasses of sweet tea. She saw Klara smiling as she stayed glued to the window. She had never seen her as radiant as she was now, even covered in muck. She knew the girl was already too far gone, and for a split second, she was worried. Worried that Klara was going to get her heart broken by another one of those useless men out there that she seemed to pick up. She knew enough about Klara's ex-boyfriends to know that she was bad at picking them. She had seen the hurt in Klara's eyes when things ended. Klara was a lot like her. Ms. May pretended to be tough, but she was a big softie inside. She wouldn't ever let anyone see that though. Never. And neither would Klara. No sign of weakness from either of them because what good would that do?

The two women walked back outside and set the tea down on the steps.

"Come take a break, child. Let me get a closer look atcha. Come on over here and sit by Ms. May. Klara said you got some questions for me? Because I got some for you, too."

Klara tensed up, not knowing where this was going but already suspicious. She knew this old lady was up to something.

"I do. I was going to ask you about life here when you were younger. What you remember about your grandparents' lives, the city and how it's changed. Your particular struggles in the city. That sort of thing," Chris said as he used his shirt as a rag and mopped the sweat from his face and chest.

The women, taking long sips of their sweet tea, sat, mesmerized as he grabbed his own glass and tipped it up. The beads of moisture dripped down his chest, trailing down his navel and stopping at his pants. Klara was breathing heavy again.

Ms. May settled in to answer Chris's questions. The three of them sat, chatting for far longer than Klara had intended. Ms. May was only too happy to share her ups and downs and all-arounds. It wasn't often she got to talk about herself, so she indulged and made the most of it.

At least two hours had passed when Klara heard the quiet rumbling of thunder in the distance. She excused herself to finish the last two houses and let Chris and Ms. May continue their conversations.

By the time she made it back to fetch the cart and Chris, the rain had already started to fall.

"Gotta go, Ms. May! Looks like you won't have to water these today!" she said hurriedly as she motioned for Chris to follow her.

The rain started to come down harder.

"Don't be a stranger, baby!" Ms. May called to Chris as he ran down the street after Klara.

He caught up with her as she was pushing the cart into the garden shed. The other volunteers had long since gone, the street quiet, except for the sound of the thunder. A loud crack made them both jump and head inside the tiny shed, laughing. The wind picked up and rattled the rotting wood that barely held the shack together.

"Think we can make a run for it to the car?" Klara said, growing quiet as she noticed the way he was looking at her.

He looked like a lion about to devour his prey. The rain started to pour down, drowning out whatever it was she had been trying to say before he kissed her. It wasn't just a soft, leaning-in peck of a first kiss. Chris put his arm around her waist and the other on the back of her head and pulled her in for an embrace before stopping to look in her eyes for a split second. Then, it was full-on, hot, lusty, heavy-breathing, mouths-opened, movie-ending kissing.

"I'm sorry. I'm sorry. I should have asked first. I ... just ... you ... "

"Do it again," she whispered.

Chris pushed her up against the shed wall, his hand slipping up the edge of her wet thigh. All the way up under her shorts until he found the curve of her ass. He kept it there as he firmly grabbed her, making Klara gasp. She ran her hands along his shoulders and down, raking her nails ever so lightly against the firmness of his back. She could feel him harden against her.

Nope, definitely not a gherkin, she thought.

They stayed in the shed, making out and feeling each other up like teenagers until the rain no longer drowned out their desires, and an awkward silence hung in the air.

"Whoa, where did that come from?" Chris said, stepping back and running his hands through his hair.

"What do you mean, where did that come from? You kissed me! You're the troublemaker."

Chris laughed before he caught eye of her serious face. "That's not what I meant. I mean ... I don't know what overcame me. You just set me on fire!"

"You're my instructor. I shouldn't have responded the way I did. I lost control of myself, too, I guess."

"It's not like I'm your professor, Klara! I'm just here to teach a quick workshop. There's no rule against what we just did."

"What did we just do?"

"I don't know. It was like a magnet was pulling me to you. I've been watching you all day, and I've been aching to just kiss you. I really didn't mean for it to go that way today. Are you upset?"

"No, I'm not upset. Not at all. I hadn't expected it either, but it was nice." Klara smiled.

"It was. Very nice," he said, taking her hand and leading her outside.

They both giggled as they headed toward Klara's car. She grabbed some towels from the trunk, drying off while discussing the residents' stories. The ride home was much different than the ride there. Both Klara and Chris kept awkwardly interrupting each other, and it seemed to Klara that there were a lot of dead silences in between their conversations. Neither knew what to say to the other, and the sexual tension still hung thick in the air between them.

"Klara, I really am sorry for that back there," Chris said as she pulled up to the hotel entrance.

"Chris! It's no big deal! Really. It was just a bit of fun. Doesn't mean a thing!" Klara thought her voice might have sounded a little too high-pitched, giving away her lingering excitement.

"Nope, doesn't mean a thing," he replied back, his voice trailing off. "Would you still like to do the observation? I understand if not."

"Of course, you doofus," Klara said, trying to lighten the mood. She wasn't sure what had gone wrong, but she could feel the sadness overcome the both of them.

"Doofus! Are you kidding me? Is that my nickname?"

"Ha! No! I'm still working on that."

"I'll expect it by the end of our observation. Tomorrow at seven work?"

"That'll work. Just tell me where I need to be."

"Here at the hotel. It's a beautiful place with lots of different people milling about. See you in the lobby at seven," Chris said before quickly waving good-bye and running off.

Klara hadn't even gotten a chance to respond before he was gone. She'd thought they would be heading back to the river or to a nearby bar. Not where he was sleeping. Not where there was a bar and a bed. Not …

Oh, to hell with it.

She drove home in silence. The scene in the shed replaying in her memory over and over. *Did I really put my hand there? Did he really moan like that into my mouth? Did my leg hike up onto his hip? Dayum.* She went over every single detail in her mind. She could feel her heart rate quicken.

She'd had made out with plenty of guys before, but never had her lust overtaken her like that. In the middle of a shed! She'd never done anything or felt anything like that. And then she remembered the sadness in the car that had washed over them both. She had been as blindsided by the sadness as she was by the passion. *Why do I feel like this? What the hell is going on with me?* She was a headstrong woman; she didn't have time for feelings.

Klara pulled into her drive. Her brain was on autopilot as she showered, put her pajamas on, took out her iceberg ice cream, and sat on the sofa. It was Saturday night, and here she was again, alone. This usually didn't bother her, but tonight, she was missing him. She thought she must be crazy. She barely knew him, and yet here she was. He was all she had thought about since she dropped him off. She couldn't let him in her head like that. She had goals and hopes and dreams, and none involved the drama of the dating world. She wasn't ready for another one to waste her time or break her heart.

Klara threw the ice cream in the trash and turned the TV off. Her mind speeding through so many thoughts and emotions. She sat at her desk and opened her laptop, and the words came flowing out. For the next six hours, Klara wrote.

FOUR

Klara waited at a table in the hotel lobby. Her pen slowly tapping on the side of her glass as anxiety creeped up her spine. She couldn't believe she'd agreed to meet him here, but he was right. The aged Gothic architecture of the mezzanine, the romantic auras from the stained glass above, the smell of mahogany from another era—it was all beautiful, inspiring, and the perfect place to people-watch.

She sipped her cocktail and eavesdropped on the conversations around her. A particular couple hiding in the corner caught her interest. The man, dressed in a dark gray business suit, sat next to a woman in a form-fitting red dress. Klara could see his hand under the table, tracing along the woman's thigh. She noticed the woman's chest rise and fall as her lips parted. The couple stared at each other, smiling and seemingly forgetting they were out in public.

Klara could feel her own breathing become heavy as she observed them to see what would happen next. The man leaned in to whisper in the woman's ear as she nodded, smiling and sipping on her martini. Her legs spread a little more as the man worked his hand up her thigh, inching closer and closer to caressing between her legs. He turned his head and softly kissed her lips. Klara saw the woman's body relax, and her hands moved to grip his knees under the table. Their legs tangled together as they moved in closer to each other. They slightly pulled away, lips still parted, breathing in each other.

When Chris exited the elevator, he noticed Klara right away. The way her navy sundress clung to her curves. The skirt softly spilling over her thighs. Her long, dark hair was pulled up in a ponytail, exposing her bare shoulders and back. She sat alone at a table, biting her lip as her gaze drifted across the lobby. Curious, he snuck to the side of the bar to watch her and order himself a beer. He stood against the back of the bar, his eyes drifting back and forth between the couple and Klara's reaction. He grinned as Klara's pen tapping turned to slow, circular motions on the paper in front of her. She put her pen down and leaned into the table, slowly sipping her cocktail and arching her back. Chris licked his lips, grabbed his beer, and made his way over to her.

She caught sight of him out of the corner of her eye and quickly pulled herself together and out of her trance. She smiled as he came up behind her, leaning in to look over her shoulder and see her work. She could feel every hair on her neck rise as his body brushed up against hers. The scent of his cologne sent her back into that shed, the moment she'd put her lips on his. The way he had pushed her up against the wall, both gentle and rough.

"It looks like you haven't gotten very far at all. Have you seen anything that interests you yet?" Chris said as he slid into the chair next to her. His legs inches away from hers.

She could feel his body heat on her bare legs. Klara's face blushed as he looked from the couple and back to her, smiling.

"Ah, yes. I did actually. I'm trying to figure out that couple over there. What do you think their story is? Anniversary?"

"No way. They aren't married. At least, not to each other," Chris said, laughing. He could tell he had his work cut out for him with Klara. "Look, they both aren't wearing rings. Plus, how many married couples do you see acting like that?"

Klara nodded in agreement. *Damn, he is perceptive.* She really did need to work on her observation skills, but it was just so easy for her to get caught up in the moment and lose focus on her work. Like right now. She was ready to pounce in between the couple and ask if they wanted a third wheel.

"So, you think she's a sex worker? A prostitute? Or maybe he's a sex worker?" Klara raised her eyebrows, proud of herself for figuring it out.

Christopher nearly choked on his beer. "That isn't what I said." He coughed and shook his head. "Klara, focus. Look at the woman's expression. What do you see? How does she feel?"

"She's smiling. Blushing. Her eyes are cast down, but she looks up every so often to meet his eyes and giggle. I would say she feels pretty damn good right now."

"So, you're saying she is ... "

"Horny?"

Chris sucked in his breath and put his head in his hands. If she was going to keep talking like this, he was going to have to scoot in just a bit closer and give her his best come-hither eyes. Although he didn't think he had the best come-hither eyes. He had tried to perfect his smoldering-eye gaze in the mirror once, and he looked more like an old man trying to read the back of a cereal box without his reading glasses.

"Okay, sure. We're getting somewhere, I guess. But what do you think she is feeling in her heart, her mind, her soul?"

"Well, damn, I didn't know you wanted me to get that deep."

"It's all about grabbing the reader by the feels, Klara. People want to feel. It's up to you to deliver. Sex comes after the feels—at least, if you're writing romance. Most of the time anyway."

"Okay. Well ... she seems unsure. Like she knows what she wants, but she is shy and scared. Her mind is working against her body."

"Uh-huh. Now, do you think, if that man hired a prostitute, she would be unsure? Or do you think she would be the one whispering in his ear and rubbing his thighs? Or, if he was the prostitute ... do those really exist anyway? Aren't they called gigolos?"

"Well, if you want to stereotype sex workers ... "

"No, I don't want to stereotype sex workers." Chris stopped her. "You're going off track again. Just watch them. Study them."

Klara threw back her drink like the badass boss lady she was— or thought she was when she was drinking gin—and concentrated on the couple. She could feel herself getting warm again. She could see the woman's foot rubbing against her partner's legs. The man quickly motioned for the check, handing the waitress his card as soon as she came to their table. The woman sighed as she traced her fingers down her neck and across her collarbone. She then leaned forward and softly touched his lips. The man growled and looked around for the waitress. By the time she came back, the couple looked ready to pounce on each other. Both were breathing heavy, biting their lips, wringing their hands, and doing everything they could not to strip each other down and go at it on the table before them.

The man suddenly stood up and held out his hand for the woman to take. The woman didn't seem to hesitate any longer. She grabbed his hand as he pulled her up and into him. He kissed her hard and led her to the elevators. Klara and Chris sat, mesmerized, as the couple passed them by. The man spoke with an accent. A sexy, *here, take my panties* accent. Klara wanted to tell them to wait for her. She was coming, too.

"Are you ready?" the man said to the woman.

"Always … for you." She giggled.

"Mine," he said as he pulled her to him and firmly gripped her ass with his free hand.

"All yours." The woman looked like she was about to melt.

Everything around them looked like it was about to melt.

Damn this couple and their outrageous sexual chemistry, Klara thought. *Is this what drugs feel like?*

Klara noticed the woman grip his hand tighter to steady herself. Her eyes trusting as he led her away and into the elevator. The elevator doors weren't even shut before he had her up against the wall. There was a heated silence as both Chris and Klara gazed at the elevator doors.

"Wow," Klara said, breathless. "I don't know if I need another drink or a cigarette after that."

Chris looked glassy-eyed. "I think I'll have whatever they had. Damn."

They both laughed and tried to pull themselves together. Their thoughts scrambled.

"What the hell was that all about?" Klara asked, still clearly frazzled by what they'd just witnessed. She wasn't sure if she was jealous of the insane amount of passion she'd just seen that made her realize she wasn't shit … or if she was shocked that such a thing even existed.

"You tell me. You're the one who was supposed to be studying them," Chris said as he gazed at Klara. He wondered what her thought process was now. *Is she as heated as I am?*

"Oh, come on! How could I? Did you see what she was doing with her hand? That little move she did before she traced his lips?"

"I did ... and that was hot as hell! Did you notice he whispered to her before she did that? I bet he told her that was what he wanted her to do."

"Really? Well, damn, that *is* hot as hell!"

"Oh, so you like dirty talk?" Chris said jokingly, waiting for her reaction of mild outrage and pretending she had no idea what he was talking about. He was really starting to learn her ways—or at least, he thought he was.

"I've never actually had someone ... I mean ... why am I telling you this?" Klara knowingly took the bait.

She really hadn't ever tried dirty talk or anything much besides regular, good ole, trusty, vanilla sex. It wasn't that she didn't want to try other things, but her previous partners had mostly been fuddy-duddies in the sack. She'd once had an ex bring a blindfold to bed. It was made out of a light, sheer material. She could totally see through it, but she didn't want to ruin his effort, so she fake blinded herself and went along with it. The blindfold was itchy, and the sex was awkward, so she faked everything else, too, just to get it over and done with. That was the last kink she had ever experienced.

"Because you want your teacher to bend you over his knees and tell you what a naughty student you are." The words spilled out of Chris's mouth before he had a chance to consider that he might just kill his career. He knew he was teasing, but did she?

Klara erupted in laughter that echoed through the lobby. She picked up a napkin and dramatically fanned herself as the waitress swung by again, and Chris ordered them another round of drinks. Chris let out a sigh of relief. That was a big, stupid risk. He was going to have to remember he was the adultier adult here. Even if Klara was making his brain foggy.

"First of all, I know that's not how you talk dirty."

"Oh, it's not?"

"No, I've read all your books. I know exactly how you would talk to me if you were to ...ya know ... talk to me like that."

"Let's hear it. Try me. What would I say?"

Klara was not one to back down from a challenge, but she was also mortified to say aloud the things that were in his books and in her head. So, she tried a different approach. "Oh, how lovely your breasts look, spilling over your corset, my dear. Spread your legs, so

I can get a view of your glistening slit, wet with my essence," she said in her best manly British accent.

I can't believe I just said that. Slit? Essence? Who am I? Klara thought before she was interrupted by Chris's laughter.

His face was red and flushed from the alcohol, the sexual tension, and the extremely inappropriate conversation they were having.

"Hmm … I don't think I've written about anyone from Britain before, but nice try."

"Oh, yeah, I'm sorry. It was a western, right? You want me to do a country, redneck accent? I can go full-on redneck. Would you like that?"

By now, Klara was three cocktails deep and obviously growing more comfortable with Chris. If she didn't quit while she was ahead, she was going to start talking about philosophies of cosmology or unicorn farts. She decided to cut herself off. Maybe. In a minute.

"I have no doubt in my mind that you can go full-on redneck."

"What the heck is that supposed to mean?"

"It means that I know Southern women. And you are as delightful and sweet as you can be. Bless your heart." Chris tried to save himself. Recovering quickly as her stare started to send laser beams through his eyes, down his body, reaching inside to punch his testicles.

"Ya better watch what ya say thar, darlin', before I give ya somethin' to fill that pretty lil' mouth of yores," Klara said, not missing a beat.

They both laughed, unable to catch their breath for several minutes.

Is this real life?

Klara was actually having a really good time, and it seemed Chris was, too.

"Aren't we supposed to be working and observing people? You're such a troublemaker, Chris," Klara teased.

"I'm completely innocent! It was you who came on to me in that shed!"

Well, damn. That escalated quickly, Klara thought. A look of shock overcame her face as she realized he had gone there. *Not only is he bringing that up, but he is also blaming me? Oh, hell no.*

"I most certainly did not!"

"I know; I know. I'm kidding. I'm the instigator. I take full credit for that. But ... about that shed," Chris said. A look of seriousness on his face. "I'm really sorry about that, Klara. I'm having a lot of fun with you, and I don't want what happened to make class awkward or ruin what little time I have left in Memphis."

"How much longer do you have? When do you leave?" Klara ignored the shed incident for now, sobered by the fact that Chris was leaving soon. She didn't know why she'd thought he wouldn't. She knew he didn't live here. She knew it wasn't forever or even for long. Why was she getting emotional all of a sudden? And then it hit her. That familiar sadness that hung in the air between them in the car when she dropped him off yesterday.

She looked at Chris, and his laugh had faded into a frown, too.

"As soon as the workshop ends. Two weeks. I've got to be in Cali for a few weeks and then back to New Orleans, and then, hopefully, Marcy, my assistant, has me scheduled for some time at home. I need to check on that."

"Oh. I see. We'd better get you some tours going then! That isn't very long to experience all Memphis has to offer. I can set you up with some friends who can help you out if you'd like?" Klara said, trying to sound happy and smiling, but she couldn't shake the sadness out of her voice.

"I was hoping you would help. Can you show me around some more? I promise I won't get weird again. I'll behave. I feel so bad about that. I hope you don't think I—"

"I liked you getting weird, Chris. No hard feelings. I wanted it, too, or else I wouldn't have responded the way I did. And, of course, I'll help you with your research. Isn't that what we're supposed to be doing now?"

"We are. Let's make the most of these two weeks. Let's have fun, live life fully in Memphis, and kick some ass on our projects."

Klara smiled but couldn't muster up any more laughs. Both of them were completely sobered up after the reality of their situation was put out in the open.

Did he bring up the fact that he was leaving to keep me from getting my hopes up? Does he think I'm falling for him? Am I? Why does he seem sad, too, if he's the one pushing back? It's just him pushing back, right? Klara thought too much. Her mind was always on everything, except what was right in front of her. She resigned herself to try to just be in the present these next two weeks. No worries, no schedules, just see where living took her.

"Deal. Partners in crime," she said as she put her hand out to shake and seal the deal.

He slowly took it and held on a little longer than just a friendly handshake.

"So, the couple, they just met, you think?" she continued as she tried to get their minds back to work.

"Maybe, but it looked to me like they knew each other pretty well. Like maybe they'd met at work and had all this tension building up, and finally, they were at a point they could do something about it. Or maybe they'd met on a dating site."

"Or ... secret swingers! Maybe they are swingers who fell in love, and they are having their first encounter together ... and alone."

"Now, you're talking! See? I knew you had it in you. Let's come up with some names and traits for these characters. Swingers, huh? Are you going to read this one aloud in class?" Chris said, thankful that the mood had lifted once again.

"I wouldn't want to get you all hot and bothered with my sexy impressions," Klara teased as they got back to work.

They worked through two more rounds of cocktails, three bottles of water, four restroom breaks, and countless pages in her notebook. Writing, changing their minds, rewriting. By the time they looked up, exhausted, the lobby was nearly empty. Klara's alarm went off on her phone.

The notification read, *You'd better have your ass in bed!*

"Oh, wow. It's eleven!"

"Why do you have an alarm for eleven?" Chris said, rubbing his eyes and stretching.

"I have alarms for everything. They help me keep on track, on schedule. How do you not have them with your busy schedule?" Klara said. She was mentally exhausted and ready to crawl into bed.

"I can't be tied down to an alarm or anything really. I need my mind to wander. It helps my work. Hey! We made a deal! Two weeks of having fun, right? Why don't you turn those alarms off for two weeks and let yourself get off track a bit? Try it my way just this once, and let's see if it helps in your writing, too."

Klara gasped at the idea. "You want me to get off schedule? You know I have a degree I'm working on, I work at the gardens, and I have a novel I'm trying to write!"

"I have a lot, too! It was just a suggestion. You don't have to. I just thought two weeks of letting yourself go would mean not being shackled to alarms and schedules and all."

"Who said I'd be letting myself go? How would I get up in the morning and be on time?"

She wondered how Chris knew this was what she'd told herself she would do when they made the deal. She did want to let herself go. She needed to let herself go, but she was almost positive she was defeated already. *How can I just forget my responsibilities?*

"Bad choice of words. I meant, just you living fully. You can still set an alarm to get up for school and work, silly! I wasn't asking you to change your entire life. Just relax a bit but still do your thing."

"Fine. I'll try it your way," she said, taking out her phone and turning off every single alarm she had set, except her morning one.

"Wow, how many do you have?"

"Depends on the day." She yawned.

They both got quiet as they stood to gather up their things and say their good-byes. The sadness washing over them once again. By now, Klara knew she liked Chris. Not just liked, but really, really liked. She wasn't sure, but she thought he felt the same. The chemistry between them had been running hot since the gardening trip. Every brush up against each other, every time they locked eyes, every blush, every tingle, every everything. She had never experienced anything like this before. It scared her, and maybe it scared him a little, too.

He's only here for two weeks. Don't do it. Don't let yourself get involved.

She tried pulling away, but it was like separating magnets. She could see he was struggling, too. He stood a little too close to her, a little too long, embraced her with a good-bye hug that he clearly didn't want to end.

"What if I stay?" she whispered, barely audible for her to even hear herself say. *Did I really just invite myself to stay the night with him?* She couldn't believe this was happening. *Is this how I let myself go?* She hoped so.

Walls up? Check. Shame out the window? Check. Caution to the wind? Check. Letting myself go? Planning on it. Klara's thought process was teetering on the edge of giving no fucks … to get a fuck.

Chris let out a long sigh of relief, cupped her face with both of his hands, and lightly kissed her on the lips. "Are you sure?"

"Yes, I'm sure! I made a deal to live life fully these next two weeks, didn't I?"

He kissed her again, pulling back long enough to look into her eyes and smile before he whispered in her ear, "I want to pin your wrists down on the mattress while you wrap your legs around me. I want your eyes on mine as we lie still, feeling each other pulsing as I slip inside you. I need to feel your heartbeat against mine, all hard throbs matching my long, rough thrusts as I dive deeper and deeper into you. I want your moans—mine. I want your body—mine. I want you—mine. Would you like that?"

Klara stood frozen. *Fuck yes, dirty talk.*

She wasn't sure what had come over Chris, but she also wasn't sure she cared to figure it out either. Her toes curled as his eyes flashed at her, darkening. Klara saw her reflection in them. She looked small and anxious, like helpless prey about to be devoured. He was hungry, and she was, too. She had no idea what was happening or how it was happening so fast, but she was determined to let it happen.

Chris grabbed her hand and led her to the elevators. Her growing desire made her even more impatient than usual as they waited and waited and waited on the slowest damn elevators this side of the planet. Chris, sensing her restlessness, pushed the elevator button again and again. He paced the floor back and forth, pausing only to pull her into him for a kiss. Finally, the doors parted, and they stepped through. He turned her around so that she could see herself in the mirrored walls of the elevator and pushed himself up against her. She could feel him harden through his pants. She grinned at their reflection as he gently tugged her ponytail to the side and nibbled her neck.

Take that, sexy swinger couple! she thought.

By the time the elevator dinged, Klara was trembling. He took her hand and quickly pulled her down the hall, only stopping to fumble with his room key. Once inside, they didn't even bother to turn on the lights. Chris kicked the door shut with his foot and began unzipping her dress. Klara's breath became raspy as she unbuckled his pants and slipped her hands under his boxers. Her hand barely wrapped around his thick cock. She could feel it pulsing as she stroked his entire length up and down. Her hand slowly becoming wet with his drips.

"You're such a naughty girl. So damn naughty," he moaned as he picked her up and took her to the bed.

He paused, hovering above her. The neon lights glowing through the window illuminated every mesmerizing curve of her body. Chris licked his lips before crawling down her body, slowly kissing every inch of her. She could feel the heat of his breath as he made his way between her legs, kissing her thighs and working his way in. His tongue licking her entirely from top to bottom.

"You taste so fucking good, Klara," he said as he pulled her hips into his face.

She ran her hands along his hairline as she watched him suck herself into his mouth and growl. Her knees quivered, and her back arched as she was quickly beginning to lose herself.

"Mmm, not yet, honey. I'm not done tasting every inch of you," he said between breaths. His hands wrapped around her thighs, steadying her to the bed as she ground against his face.

"I need you inside me. Now!" she urged as she pulled him up to her face.

He kissed her hard as he pinned her wrists above her head. Whatever rabid emotions took over Klara, she wouldn't be surprised if she started foaming at the mouth.

His mouth. His delicious, dirty, filthy mouth.

She could taste herself on his lips.

"Look at me. I want to see your eyes that moment I first slip inside you." Chris paused long enough to let Klara buck against him, begging for him to fill her up.

Her cheeks flushed pink, her breath wavering. She moaned, her hips rising to meet him, restless. She needed to feel him inside her. He leaned over and reached for a condom from the nightstand drawer, tearing the foil with his teeth and rolling it on in one swift motion.

"Are you ready? I bet you feel so damn good, Klara."

Chris held her tight as he slowly—very, very slowly—slid right inside her wetness. She gasped and hooked her legs around his waist, positioning herself so that he ground against her clit with each thrust. She reached behind her to grip the headboard. She had to have something to hold on to. She felt like she was going to fall off the edge of the world.

Feeling her body start to tremble, Chris started to quicken his pace. His rhythm matched hers as they both let themselves go. They tangled themselves together, melting into each other. Not knowing where one body started and the other ended.

They rocked back and forth together. Their bodies in sync. Their moans in sync. Their breaths in sync. Their orgasms in sync as a warm tingle overtook them, sending waves of pleasure rippling through them.

Klara lay still, throbbing, as Chris remained on top of her, kissing her shoulders, her neck, her lips before lying down next to her. She turned to face him, running her hands along his chest, arms, and those abs that made her feel so damn dizzy. His abs were a work of art. He was a work of art. From his chiseled build to his beautiful mind. Klara was falling, fast. She wondered if he was, too. She couldn't let herself get hurt. Not this time, not anytime.

"I guess I'd better go," she said, slowly rising from what felt like a dream. She needed to pinch herself. She needed to wake up, but then again, she didn't want to wake up.

"Go? I thought you were staying?" Chris sounded offended. "Did I do something wrong?"

"No, not at all! I just know we have to both be up for class in the morning, and I thought ... I don't know. Isn't that what I am supposed to do after? Leave?"

"After? I was just getting started! And I definitely don't want you to go anywhere. Stay with me. We can set your alarm for a little earlier for you to swing by your house and get ready."

"Are you sure? Won't you be too tired to teach in the morning?"

"Am I sure? Jeez Louise! I have a gorgeous woman in my bed. And I would love to fuck her brains out. Again ... and again ... and again. Do you really think I want you to go?"

"Did you just say, 'Jeez Louise'? Is that like old geezer talk? Can we go back to the filthy language?"

"Ha! I think I'm supposed to be bending you over my knee for being a naughty student, isn't that right?"

"Yes. I have been pretty naughty, haven't I?" she said, turning to meet his gaze.

His eyes took her all in. Her slender thighs, her swollen pink lips—both sets. Her nipples, hard and tingling, ready for him to reach out and touch her again. He looked at her for what seemed like forever. Long enough to make her start to feel self-conscious or that something was wrong with what he was seeing.

"You are so damn beautiful, Klara. Every. Single. Bit of you. I want to spend every moment I can with you. I wouldn't want us to leave the room if we didn't have to. Now, get back down here and let me teach you a lesson," Chris said as he grabbed her hand and pulled her back down to the bed.

Klara could feel herself becoming a puddle in his hands.

They were lust-drunk. Both falling—and fast. This couldn't end well.

FIVE

Chris paced the floor as he gave his lecture. His demeanor was professional without a hint of the dirty lover he'd portrayed last night. His calm voice steady and reassuring the students of their successes. Nothing like the growly boss man who had been whispering in Klara's ear just hours ago.

What I wouldn't give to have him on that desk, Klara thought.

Their rendezvous had left her a little sore and very tired. She was sore in places that she hadn't even known could ache. She smiled to herself as she tried to sit comfortably in the desk. Each pang in her muscles sending her back into her memories and back into his arms. She was still smiling when she looked up and noticed everyone was gone, except Chris.

"What's the smile for?" he said as he approached her desk. "Watching musclemen porn on that laptop?"

"No way! Who do you think I am? Besides, that's not the kind of porn I watch." Klara grinned. She wanted him. Again. Today. Tonight. Tomorrow. Now. *What the hell is wrong with me?* She was insatiable.

"Oh, it's not? Well, what kind of porn do you watch? Tell me what you like," Chris said, his eyebrows raised.

The halls were calm and quiet. The only sound in the room was the sound of their breaths. Klara frantically tried to steady her breathing as her heart rate began to rise.

Am I breathing too loud? Too fast?

He was going to think she was having an asthma attack if she didn't get herself under control. That was not very sexy. Code red for the silly schoolgirl with the teacher crush. Her palms started to sweat.

"Oh, you know, just the regular vanilla stuff. I'm not very interesting," Klara lied. What kind of porn didn't she watch? Oh, well, yeah, there was that stuff her ex David was into. *No. Way. What was that even called again? A hot carl? A hot pocket? A steaming Alabama? A pocket ball?* She could feel herself getting nauseous as her mind wandered down this path.

"I don't believe that for a second. And … I think you're very interesting. But that's okay. You can tell me more about this porn habit over lunch. What do you say?"

"I *do not* have a porn habit!" Klara's face was starting to turn pink. She could feel her cheeks getting warm and flushed.

Is he serious?

She could never tell with Chris. He was such a tease. One minute, she wanted to cross her arms and deliver him the evil eye; the next minute, she wanted to spread her legs and deliver him the bad mamma jamma. Mamma jamma. He was turning her into a sex fiend. An awkward, goofy, drunken-on-him sex fiend.

"So … I take it that is a yes?" he asked.

He smiled, noticing her brain clearly wasn't functioning this morning. He knew why. His brain had barely caught up from last night's events, too. All morning, his mind had been on the way her hair had framed his face as she leaned down to kiss him. The view of her perfect, bouncing breasts and her parted pink lips as she had thrown her head back in ecstasy while her hips ground into him. Several times, he could feel himself start to harden. He quickly had to think of something, anything, before that happened. He had been in the middle of speaking about colloquiums to the class when he noticed himself start to rise yet again. His thoughts frantic, trying to stop the rise of his need. His need for *her*.

The xy=bc and the square root of something is the third law of motion? Isaac Newton naked? Isaac Newton standing butt naked, writing his laws of motion on a chalkboard while his wrinkled old-man ass hangs, melting off his back? Fuck, that's nasty!

Chris's desire stifled as he brought himself back to reality. He was going to have to remember that naked Newton was a surefire way to make his cock shrivel like a raisin. Poor thing. He would need to make sure it was okay the first chance he got.

"Yeah, I'll take some lunch. I have just the place for you. It's an old brothel turned into a greasy burger bar."

"Oh my. You sure do know the way to my heart," he said before realizing he said it. *Heart.*

She was going to think he was love-struck. She was going to think he was a stage five clinger. That one romp in the sack was enough to send him hugging her legs and begging her not to leave him. How unattractive.

He cleared his throat and straightened himself up, sensing the awkwardness that followed his *heart.* "I mean, I'm always down for some greasy food! And I would love to see an old brothel. Perfect place for some of my research. Now, if you'd please quit watching that Sasquatch porn, let's go. I'm starving!"

"Damn it, you caught me!" She laughed as she packed her belongings up.

Her mind was racing and still on the fact that he'd totally said she knew the way to his heart. Clogged arteries and bawdy ladies? Probably. Typical American male. She made a mental note to dress like a call girl and take him out for steaks before he left. Maybe that would do it.

Do what? What exactly am I trying to do? Klara was still unsure what she wanted.

She'd thought she knew what she wanted. She was happy enough, living in her own little world and working on her own little things. That was up until she'd met Chris. And, now, she was confused as to what she wanted. He would be leaving soon, and long-distance relationships never worked. Besides, she was probably just a plaything to him while he was here. Except she wasn't. She sensed it. She knew the way to his *heart.* He'd said so himself.

The restaurant was packed with the usual Memphis mix. Old, young, hipster, geezer. Everyone laughing and smiling, everyone having a good time. Klara loved her city. The people here knew how to have fun. The struggles of day-to-day living were relatable to them all. And they all had the frame of mind to say screw it and have a good time in life despite all the bullshit life threw at them. She observed Chris as he took in the surroundings. His face alight as he soaked up the tattered walls, the worn-out bar, the advertisements tacked on the windows. Party here and party there.

"Well, what do you think?" Klara said, taking a bite of her greasy burger. She was going to regret eating this. She'd skipped her run this morning because she had exercised all night. *Wink, wink.* But this burger was going to make her run ... to the restroom. She could basically swim in the grease. It was as if she were lubing her insides, preparing for ... *tentacle porn?* Why was she thinking about porn still? Was it because Chris was sitting in front of her and doing that thing? You know, that thing he did—living, breathing, anything he did. Because it all sent her into a state of bedroom bliss.

"I think it's fascinating! Can you imagine the stories in these walls?" he said, taking in his surroundings.

"I know! If these walls could talk, what do you think they would say?"

"Clean me. I've been a dirty whore."

"Ha! I see what you did there!" Klara laughed.

He was right though. The walls were caked in grime and grease and probably many other things from way back when.

"It's all part of that Southern charm. Dirty South, right?" Klara continued. "Anyway, what's island life like? Where is your island again? Do y'all have these kinds of places down there?"

"We have a few beach shacks that I guess you could call dive bars but nothing like this," he said, motioning around the crowded room. "Captiva is in South Florida," Chris continued. "It's very small and very slow. There isn't much to do there, except bike, fish, boat. For nightlife, we have to head into Florida, the Fort Myers area. It's a great place to write because there isn't much else to do. And, plus, you have the beach, which is always nice and inspiring."

"South Florida! I've never heard of Captiva. I thought you lived in the Bahamas or something," Klara said, breathing a sigh of relief.

South Florida wasn't too far, *and* it was drivable. It wouldn't be like she would have to take a boat across the ocean. So, he wouldn't be long, long-distance at least. She let this sink in her mind as he rambled on about life at the beach.

"It's a great getaway, but sometimes, it does get boring, and that's when my love of travel comes in. I think you would like it though. You should come down sometime." The words escaped Chris's mouth before he had a chance to think about what he was asking. It must have been his damn heart talking again.

He really did want her to come see his place though. The beach and Klara in an itty-bitty bikini? Damn right! He wondered what kind of bikini she would wear. Black? White? Red? He was imagining a type of floral pattern, surely. He was going to have to backtrack on this somehow before she thought he wanted to walk down the aisle.

"The beach, huh?" Klara smiled. She was pretty sure her heart was in her throat, or it was that last bit of burger she'd finished. That wouldn't be good.

"Well, yeah. Maybe you could get some work done. I'm hardly ever there. You'd have the place to yourself!"

What the heck? Klara thought.

She could have sworn he was asking her to go with him to the beach, *not* stay at his house when he wasn't even there. Maybe he was just being friendly then. She was going to have to set some boundaries and guard herself before this got any deeper.

"I could use some peace and quiet. I'll keep that in mind. Thanks!"

"Anytime, Klara."

They both finished their food, and Klara grabbed the check before Chris could get out his wallet. She was adamant on treating him today. She was the one who'd wanted to take him here. She didn't need a white knight. Chris didn't seem too happy about her paying the check, but his chivalry was going to have to wait. He could see Klara's stubbornness wouldn't budge.

"Fine. You paid for lunch; I got dinner. But you'll have to wait. I've got just the place in mind, but I'll need reservations. You free on Friday?" Chris's voice was a little too high as he asked. *Why does this woman make me so damn nervous? I just had my head between this woman's legs. Why am I all of a sudden stammering like a terrified child?*

"Are you asking me on a real date?" Klara intently looked at Chris. As if she was trying to read his thoughts and what he was up to.

What kind of joke is this? Is this just some observing session? Is he just horny? Am I supposed to wait until Friday to get in his pants again? That's not going to work.

"As a matter of fact, yes. I would love to take you on a real date."

And he had done it again. He'd said the L-word this time. No way he could be in love. It wasn't possible to have love at first sight. He wrote about all that stuff, but he didn't believe in it. Besides, she was a student with a big future blah, blah, blah. He was an old man with a questionable future in writing at the moment. Maybe his Memphis book would pull him out of the slump. Especially if he channeled some of this—whatever this was—into it.

Limerence? Yes! It's just limerence! Chris congratulated himself on coming to that conclusion. No crazy love eyes here. Just some good old-fashioned limerence. That was why he couldn't get enough of Klara. What a relief that was to have passed on all those feels! Now, he could enjoy her without that nagging feeling that he was falling too deep. You couldn't fall too deep with limerence. It was just a science thing in the brain. Chemicals or some crap. Not the real deal. He was all good. *Phew.*

"I would love to!" And, now … she'd said it.

Klara, Klara.

Klara could picture her mom wagging her finger in her face. What a fool she was being. Giving up the milk. Being a cow. Being free? Something like that. She had let her guard down, and now, she was going on a real date. That hadn't happened in what seemed like forever. If he was asking her out, that meant he liked her, right? Maybe she wasn't just a plaything. Maybe he was willing to put in some work to make this happen. How would they? How could they?

"So, where are you taking me?" she said. She knew it must be a historical place. Somewhere he probably wanted to go anyway for some research.

"It's a surprise! Wear something dressy. I'll handle the rest."

"Oou, Mr. Big Shot. Okay."

"Is that my nickname? Mr. Big Shot?" Chris teased. "You promised you would give me one. Let's hear it."

"No, it's not Mr. Big Shot. I actually don't have one for you. I really don't. Which is super odd because they usually come easy to

me. So, I guess you'll just have to be a regular ole Chris to me!"
Klara said, shrugging her shoulders.

She had tried to come up with something that wasn't cheesy,
but Crude Chris, Filthy-Mouthed Chris, Cutie Chris, Chris in My
Mouth. None of those worked. McChris, Chris McMuffin, Christo-
fiend. She was at a loss for words. He was just going to have to be
her Chris.

"I'll just wait. I'm sure something will come to you." He
winked at her.

Didn't he know that, when a man winked at a woman, it
automatically made her panties drop a lil' bit? Just a smidge. She
wanted him to wink again. Get them down around her ankles.

Why did men ever quit winking in the first place?

Klara hadn't had anyone wink at her in years. Men her age
preferred the chin-up nod that looked like a quick sniff of the air,
as if to say, *Your pheromones are making my balls tingle.* But, in actuality,
these "men" probably had no idea what a pheromone was, and the
tingles were probably from something they should talk to their
doctor about. Just one of the many reasons she gravitated toward
the older fellows.

"Oh, wait! We didn't go check out the upstairs. That's where
the rooms are!" She remembered as they stood to leave.

"Rooms?" Chris said, dazed from either a food coma or the
hustle and bustle of the downtown lunch hour.

"You know … the rooms the patrons rented … by the hour,"
she said, wiggling her eyebrows and sending them both into a fit of
laughter.

He flagged down the waitress and asked if they could take a
quick peek upstairs.

"Of course you can! We usually keep that area roped off, but
since you're interested, I think I can pull a few strings," said the
flirty waitress who obviously knew all too well who Christopher
Kaiser was. Her hand softly patting his shoulder and staying
there—for forever.

"Is that how you flirt? The eyebrow thing?" Chris said as they
made their way up the stairs.

Klara kept climbing until she reached the top. A barely lit,
narrow hallway lined with old wooden benches awaited them. She
took Chris's hand and led him to a bench.

"No, this is how I flirt," she said as she cradled his face with her hands and pulled his lips into hers.

Well, she had told herself that she couldn't wait until Friday. At least she was honest with herself. *Why wait?* She had eleven days left with Chris. She was going to have to spend at least eleven of them in bed.

"That is certainly better than the spastic brows, but I think I'll take them both. Show me again how you flirt. Flirt real hard for me," he said as he sat on the bench and pulled Klara on top of his lap.

The hallway was quiet, save for the echoing soft moans escaping Klara's mouth. She looked around, nervous that anyone could pop out of one of the rooms. All the doors were closed, and by the looks of it, no one had been up here in a while. There was even a faint layer of dust on the floor.

"Shh," he said, sensing her anxiousness. "We'll be able to hear the stairs creaking if anyone comes up."

Klara nodded her head, reassured, and went back to his lips. She could feel him harden underneath her as she straddled his lap. She rocked her hips back and forth, rubbing her clit against the length of his hard cock.

Her panties were starting to get wet as he whispered into her ear, "You want me to fuck you in this whorehouse, Klara? Would you like that? Can you come for me like you're my dirty little whore?"

And that was all he needed to say before she was back in ravenous mode.

Who knew I liked dirty talk so much? If anyone else ever called her a whore, she would usually cut them, but Chris ... oh, she loved being Chris's whore. Whore, girlfriend, wife—she'd take it. Take him. And she did.

Chris fumbled with his pants zipper, pulled himself out, and hastily slipped a rubber over his throbbing cock. Klara lifted up as he pulled her skirt up and pushed her panties to the side, and then she guided herself back down onto him. He let out a moan as she leaned down to kiss him again. His hands gripped her hips, pulling them into him and pushing them back out. Showing her the pace he liked. She circled her hips, watching him start to lose himself. Chris couldn't take it anymore. He had to have his way with her. He needed to have her up against the wall.

He picked her up, grabbing her ass hard as he walked her over to the wall. Her arms and legs wrapped around him as he thrust against her. Klara moaned loudly. Her mouth inches from his. Chris put his hand over her mouth and saw her eyes roll back.

"You're so fucking hot. I'm so glad you're mine. All mine," he said, slamming into her over and over. "I want you to come for me, okay?" he whispered, his hand still on her mouth, keeping her from getting too loud and giving them away. Their moans were stifled as he buried his mouth into her neck, biting her while she dug her heels into his hips.

Chris caught the look in her eyes. The same look she'd made last night right before she reached orgasm. He could fill her gripping his cock. She was almost there.

"Come for me, Klara. I want to feel us dripping down your thighs. God, you feel so fucking good. I fucking love the way you pulse around me. You're so warm. So wet. I'm going to lose myself in you, my sweet girl."

She bit down hard on his hand as he felt her inner muscles tighten and release in waves. His rock-hard cock erupted inside her, matching her rhythm again. Their bodies were in sync as they pushed themselves into the wall. Exhausted, spent, and a little disoriented, they both started to giggle.

"Thanks for the dessert!" he said as he steadied himself against the wall.

Klara's knees were shaking as she clumsily made her way back to the bench.

"That ... was my pleasure. Wow, dirty whore, huh? Damn. Where did that even come from?"

"I'm so sorry! Did that offend you? I didn't mean it like that. I just thought ... well, we were here, and you'd seemed to like it when I was talking dirty last night ... I really didn't mean to upset you."

Klara laughed as she got to her feet and made her way over to him. She placed her hand on him, cupping him through his jeans.

"Actually, I did like it. I'm not offended at all! Trust me, if I'm offended, you'll know about it!"

"I have no doubt in my mind that I will," he said, still catching his breath.

The crowd was dying down as the two made their way downstairs. Much less drinking and cursing and more moans and laments of gastrointestinal regrets. The breath of fresh air as they stepped outside was a relief.

"Ahh, sunshine and blue skies! Where to next, my little tour guide?" He winked. Again.

She was going to have to put some sunglasses on him to block his gaze that seemed to look straight into her soul. *Can he see my soul? Am I wearing my heart on my sleeve—again?* She suddenly seemed uncomfortable. *What if he can tell how I feel?* His deep stare made her face feel awkward. *Am I doing something crazy with my eyes? Is my face twitching?*

She would have to put on sunglasses for herself to hide behind.

"Are you okay?" Chris said, his head cocked to the side like a good puppy, wondering what trickery this was. "Are you flirting again, Ms. Eyebrows?"

"Ah, nope. Had something in my eye. Let's go! I've got just the place for us!" Klara took her gigantic bug-eye sunglasses out of her glove compartment and put them on. Half of her face was now covered up. She felt invisible.

There's no way his eyes can penetrate these glasses! Penetrate ... Chris ...

She shook her head to try to get rid of her naughty thoughts and headed out to give Chris a tour of her city. What she really had in mind was no more stupid ideas, like going to the brothel. *What was I thinking?* Of course that would be sexy. Sneakily fucking in the open in a closed-off section, upstairs in an old brothel? Um, yes, please!

She had to slow down and try to be more hospitable and less slutty. So, naturally, she took him to the old cemetery. What could be sexy about that? She was sure there would be no hanky-panky-spanky when they had the heebie-jeebies, and she was right. Both of them found themselves immersed in so many stories of local legends that they forgot the time. The sun was already setting by the time they returned to the car.

"Wow. Thanks for taking me here! That was amazing! I got a lot of good information out of that. I'm going to be up all night, writing."

"It was my pleasure, Chris. I've actually been writing more, too. You've been good for me. In so many ways," Klara said, wiggling her eyebrows again and making them both burst into laughter.

Chris was amazed at how someone could be so beautiful, so smart, and so funny, all rolled into one package. He was a little taken aback at the awe he'd experienced throughout the day. It was perfect. The greasy dive bar/bordello had been amazing; the sneaky, knee-quivering sex had been mind-blowing; the flirty banter during the car ride had been playful; and even the sun setting over the headstones in a creepy, old cemetery had ended the day beautifully. Klara was perfect. They were perfect. *No, wait, what?*

He couldn't let this train of thought cross his path. She was perfect, yes, but she was also here … and soon, he would be there. And then what? He would go to another city, find another muse, carry on. The show must go on. But did it? He didn't want another muse. He just wanted Klara and all her quirky, stubborn-as-fuck, dripping sarcasm; her magnificent ass; her head-in-the-clouds, OCD self. But he couldn't have her. Or could he? Hell, who knew? He'd never tried a long-distance relationship, and he wasn't even sure if that was what she wanted. These feelings were all new to him. He felt old, worn out, and exhausted from the ton of bricks that he'd sweetly named limerence. Just limerence.

"I've got another proposition for you," Chris said as he tapped his chin in dramatic thought.

"Another one, huh? So, we're all caught up on our last one though, right? I showed you around; you've helped me with my writing."

"All caught up. This is something new. A goal, so to speak. You and I can hold each other accountable in our writing. Let's say, three thousand words a day. Minimum."

"That's a lot!"

"It's summer break; you don't have school. And I can help you with your work in the gardens if you'd like. I wouldn't mind another trip to see that old cougar Ms. May anyway."

"I guess I can try."

"Try? You're a writer, Klara. You just need to believe it yourself. Do you want to write together? Remember, we're supposed to be kicking ass on our project as part of the two-week deal."

Crap, Chris thought. He really was a stage five clinger. Maybe even a stage nine right now. But he just couldn't help himself. He didn't want to feel that sadness again when she left, and it was only two weeks. He could do two weeks and move on to the next city, the next muse.

"Klara," he continued, "we can be each other's muses."

"Muse, huh? I bet you call all the girls your muse," she said, halfway joking, halfway not. She meant, he had to have a ton of women all over the place. Look at him! He was gorgeous, successful, fun, flirty, and the way he'd whispered filthy things in her ear made her heart fall into her stomach when she thought about it. Like now.

Crap! Those are butterflies!

Klara hadn't had that butterfly feeling in years. She'd forgotten that feeling.

Busted, Chris thought as his face reddened. Thankfully, they had just pulled up to the hotel lobby. He ran his hands through his hair, fidgeting.

"Maybe a few here and there." He grinned, putting his hand on the lever to open the door and run as soon as she stopped the car. He didn't want to have to explain. "But none have amused me like you do, Klara." He winked.

Not the damn wink, she thought.

"I see what you did there. Clever, Chris—hey! There's a nickname idea!"

"Really? Just Clever Chris? That's not really sexy." He frowned.

"You think Farmer John is a sexy nickname? You should hear my other ones! I think you did pretty well. But, if you don't like it … I guess I can—"

"Do better. You can do better! I'll have to give you more material, I guess," Chris said as he wiggled his eyebrows and hopped out of the car.

Klara erupted in a fit of laughter. His dark eyebrows looked like two caterpillars trying to do a really awkward mating dance on his forehead. She thought she'd better not tell him that though.

"Okay, okay. I'll keep trying. When are we writing?"

"Tomorrow, after class. Does that work?" he said, leaning down and peering through the rolled-down window.

By this time, it was nightfall, and Klara had given up on hiding her expressions behind her glasses.

I'm going to need a Xanax to calm my face if he keeps this up. She rubbed her eyes, pretending to be tired.

"I'll be there." She yawned.

"Good night, Klara." Chris bowed like a gentleman as he gently shut the door.

"Good night, Chris," she called back, pulling away.

The now-familiar sadness crushed down on her. She checked the rearview mirror and saw Chris's shoulders slump as he walked through the lobby doors.

SIX

The days passed by too fast for Klara's liking. She and Chris had developed a sort of routine ever since their outing to the brothel and around town. Each morning after class, she and Chris would sneak off to the corner coffee shop to sit across from each other and write their novels. They'd both order their lattes, pop in their headphones, and race to see who could get the most writing done before lunchtime.

"On your mark …" Klara narrowed her eyes, challenging Chris from across the table.

"Get set …" he said, shooting the look right back to her.

"Go!" She giggled, already starting ahead of time.

"Cheater!" he called her out.

Klara pretended not to hear him over the sad indie music playing in her ears. The scene she was working on involved a very tragic death. She liked to tailor her music to her moods when she was writing, and this one was really bothering her. A far step down from the gangster rap that had been blaring in her ears yesterday while she wrote about a shoot-out and also a much different approach than Chris's never-ending classical piano playlist.

Chris's foot nudged Klara's under the table. Both smiling but neither looking up from their computers. They had spent the last few days enjoying this routine. Class, coffee, writing, dirty sex, lunch, and then Klara would go off to work, leaving Chris to get out and explore the city, solo. She was working the shop this week but eager to have her hands in the dirt again. Ms. May would probably give her an ass chewing for not coming around lately, but Klara had been a bit preoccupied. Not only with Sexy

McSexserson, but she had also been making real progress on her book. She was finally beginning to feel like an adult—or at least like she could get away with pretending to know what she was doing.

Although Klara was getting plenty of sexy time with Chris, she hadn't stayed the night again since that first time. She knew the familiar sadness would hit her as soon as they parted ways, and falling asleep next to him was just a cruel tease of what she couldn't have. Chris hadn't exactly offered either, which, she had to admit, bothered her a bit.

She wondered what that was all about. *Is he keeping me at a distance, too, or is it something more practical? Like does he snore? Does he sleep-fart? Ew.* One of her exes was bad about that. She had gone to bed every night with a stink face when she was with him. He was a symphony of sounds. Toots and blows and honks out of every end.

She looked up and caught Chris's gaze. *Is he falling too fast and too hard, too? Does he feel like I feel? And, if he does, why doesn't he say something, damn it? We're all adults here. Even if one of us has his shit together and is adultier than the other.* Klara's shit wasn't together at all, even with all the alarms and calendars—which, she realized, didn't make a damn bit of difference in her life when she gave that up. She still didn't live in the moment even if she'd promised Chris she would these two weeks. She was in the future, small, shivering, and wrapped up in her anxiety burrito. The sad times without him were getting harder and harder. How would she feel when he was gone for good?

Chris took his headphones out and gave Klara a little wave as he tried to get her attention. "Hey, Miss Best-Seller. How's it coming along over there?"

"Really great actually! You? Ready to compare notes? See who is the loser this round? Loser gets ... what, tied up?"

"Well, in that case, let me delete some of this," Chris said, pretending to type away on his keyboard before shutting his laptop completely. "I win."

"We haven't counted! You cheat! Let me see it!"

"I only have two words! I promise!" Chris joked.

"Fine, but tomorrow, I'm only writing two. Same prize," Klara said, trying to look serious but failing miserably at it.

"Actually, that's what I wanted to talk to you about. Tomorrow ..." Chris hesitated.

"Yeah?" Klara sat up, eager to know where this was going.

"It can be good or bad news. Your choice."

Klara's heart dropped. *What is this all about? I'm enjoying our routine, and now, he is going to mess it all up? Or make it better? Good or bad? My choice?* It didn't make sense. No one started out a conversation like that unless it was bad.

Chris ran his hands through his hair and sighed, clearly struggling to deliver the information. "I've got to go back home this weekend. I have some urgent papers that need to be signed for my dad's retirement accounts. Apparently, they can't wait."

"Okay." Klara shut her laptop. The dread and gloom were already suffocating her. "What do you mean by it being my choice? I guess that's a good thing. These papers?"

"No, that's not what I meant. Although, yeah, it's a good thing. What I'm asking you is, will you go with me? Beach trip to clear your mind? And get even more work done on your novel. Remember the deal? Live in the moment." He crossed his legs under the table, and his fingers crossed behind his back. He really wanted her to come. He needed her to come. He was completely wound up in limerence—the healthier L-word. If he could focus on this spark being limerence, not Klara, then that would make things easier when he really did have to leave for good.

"It really doesn't take much convincing for me to go to the beach, ya know. Let's do it."

"Phew. Good. I already got you a ticket. We leave tomorrow at noon."

Klara's jaw dropped. That was either an incredibly stupid move or an incredibly romantic move. What if she had said no? Yeah, right!

He hasn't even known me long, yet he totally understands me. He gets me. He loves me? She shook the thought out of her head. She was beginning to think she was a little crazy. She didn't want to be the crazy girlfriend.

Girlfriend? Ugh! Klara couldn't stop her train of thought.

She had been having so much fun the last week and didn't want it to stop. She wanted to be his.

"Does this mean our hot date night is canceled?"

"This means, our hot date night will be on the beach, watching the sunset. But, no, date night in Memphis isn't canceled. It's just postponed. Next week, before I leave." His voice trailed off. Before he left. For good.

Limerence.

"I'll double-check that I can get someone to cover for me at the shop, but I think I should be able to pull it off," Klara said, trying to focus on the beach trip and not on next Friday. Date night. How could she have a good date night the night before he left? She was going to be a mess! Maybe she would end up "sick" and not have to deal with good-byes. She would have to think of all that when the time came. For now, she had emotions to bottle up and a beach trip to pack for.

Chris didn't have the typical bachelor's pad. The art that hung on his walls was actual art and not posters of scantily clad women or abstract race-car parts. There were no beer bottles or pizza boxes strewed about. Nothing smelled funny. Everything was clean, beautiful, breathtaking even. Klara had known he did well in his career, but she'd had no idea he did this well. She felt a little out of place and exposed in such a bright, open space.

"Wow, Chris! This place is gorgeous," Klara said, still standing inside the entryway and taking in her surroundings.

Chris stood, mesmerized by her as the natural light from the skylight above shone down on her like something out of a science fiction novel. He reached behind himself to steady himself on a wall. He could watch her here all day.

It had been a long time since a woman was in his home. Too long. He hoped it wasn't too cold and sterile for Klara. All the whites and sleek edges.

Marcy had hired the designer when he bought the place two years back. His only request was she not go all HGTV farmhouse on him. If that happened, then he would put her in his next novel as a bug-eyed, wrinkled-up, old prune nobody wanted to fuck. She'd teased him by hanging a picture of a cow that first week, but he had known she would eventually come through. She always did. His home was now a work of art. He was very proud of it even if no one really ever got to see it.

"Thanks. I can't take credit for it. Marcy did that. Well, she hired someone to make it nice and keep it nice anyway. I'm not here much to enjoy it, unfortunately."

"I would never leave here if I were you, Chris. I mean, who the hell has this view?" she said as she made her way to the patio.

The surf was rough today and could be heard echoing throughout the house. He followed her out the door, grinning like an idiot behind her. He was so happy that she liked it. It really didn't appear as cold and lonely with Klara in it. She warmed everything up. It was almost as if the sunlight followed her around each room or that she was the sunlight.

"The view is what sold me. There's something about being here with a cup of coffee, watching the sunrise, or a glass of wine, watching the sunset, that inspires me to bring out my laptop and just write."

"You're living the dream," she said, her eyes still wide and awestruck.

Chris started but held back, putting his hands in his pockets instead. He was living the dream, but it was a lonely dream. He hadn't known just how lonely he was until he met Klara.

Limerence.

"Come on. Let me show you to your room."

"I get my own room?" she said as giddy as a schoolgirl.

"Only if you want it," he replied. He hoped she didn't want her own room.

"What are my options?"

"Well, let's see. We have three guest rooms, my room, the pool house, and several couches."

"I think I'll need the grand tour before I can decide," she said innocently.

He played along, saving his bedroom until last. He knew by her reaction to just the downstairs that his room would blow her mind. It still blew his each time he walked through those doors to the master bedroom. His chamber, as he liked to call it. Not a sex chamber, unfortunately. Not yet anyway.

Chris showed Klara around his home. He made sure to point out the coffeemaker because he knew she was an addict, just like he was. He pointed out the wet bar because, well, same. The beds, she tested by sitting on each one and describing them as just not comfy enough. An innocent twirl of her hair around her finger and then a puppy-dog pout. Chris was beginning to realize he really liked being teased.

"Okay, Goldilocks. Ready to try the last bed?"

"Ready!" She grinned.

They made their way to the last room, shut by double doors and nestled at the end of a very long hall.

"After you, my lady." Chris bowed, opening the door and letting her through.

She had never seen anything like it. Well, she had, but that was in the bullshit *Real Housewives* drama series. Not in real life. Not in her life anyway. The entire back wall was covered in windows that opened to its own private patio overlooking the ocean. Chris grabbed the remote beside the bed and opened them all. The sea breeze blew in, tangling the white linen that hung from his four-poster bed.

"I pick this one," she whispered, dazed as she gazed at the ocean.

He came up behind her, taking her hair in his hand and moving it to the front of her shoulders so that he could kiss the back of her neck.

"I was hoping you'd say that," he said as he picked her up and threw her on the soft feather bed.

Klara squealed as he climbed on top of her, taking one of her legs at a time and gently removing her heels.

"You look right at home in this bed, Goldilocks. Tell me, do you like it hot? Do you like it wet? Do you like it just right?" Chris ran his thumb up and down her pussy. Her legs still thrown messily over his shoulders.

"I like it hot. I like it wet. And your cock in my mouth right now would be just right."

"Fuck!" he said, caught off guard. "You're really learning some things, I see. Maybe I'm a bad influence."

"So fucking bad," she said, throwing her legs out to the sides and spreading herself wide. Her dress hiked up over her hips, her hand reaching down to tease herself.

"How about you straddle my face and show me how bad you can be?" he said, hurriedly settling in beside her and already unzipping himself. His cock stood, ready and dripping.

"I thought you'd never ask." Klara pulled her panties off and turned around, nestling herself snug on top of his mouth while leaning down to take him in her mouth at the same time. Her tongue ran the length of him as she slowly teased him.

He pulled her back further and buried his face in between her thighs, sending shivers up her spine. His hands gripped tightly on her ass, leaving little pink fingerprints. Klara lost focus, stopping what she was doing and gripping the bedsheets to steady herself.

"Naughty girl. Focus on my cock while I focus on this gorgeous pussy of yours," he said, slapping her ass hard.

She giggled and went back to work, gasping in between breaths and close to giving in to the waves overtaking her. Chris lightly ran his fingertips up and down her back while his tongue flicked back and forth across her. His hips rose as he pulled her deeper onto him. He was pulsing, about to lose himself. The warm, silky feel of her tongue twirling around the tip of him was too much to handle. He thrust his hips into her mouth and held on to her thighs, now shaking and on the verge of collapse. Both cried out through full mouths, hanging on to each other tight as their bodies released control.

Klara rolled off to his side, spent and dazed from where she was, what she was doing, who she was doing. Her fingers reached out to touch the softly swaying hanging linens. The cool breeze washing over her, too. *Is this a dream? Surely, this is a dream.* She sat up in bed, listening to the waves crash and imagining them in sync with the waves inside her.

Chris jumped out of the bed and quickly sat back down. Head rush. Klara had completely frazzled all of his senses. The way her soft lips had enclosed around him, taking every inch of him into her mouth. The way her sweet folds tasted on his tongue. The way her body shook as she got closer and closer to giving in to him. That little moment right before, where she'd held her breath and then let it all out in one loud cry. That was his favorite. He played that on repeat in his head all the damn time.

He kissed her forehead and disappeared for a quick second to grab some robes. The euphoric look on her face, making him brave or stupid. But that look … that look wasn't just an after-sex face. He had observed too many people to know. That look was pure bliss. Sing-from-the-rooftops, fight-for-your-lover, wild, reckless limerence? They hadn't even known each other long, but whatever this was they were doing, it just seemed so right. Maybe it was the dopamine, maybe it was the fresh air, or maybe it was just Klara.

But he had another proposal, and if this one didn't work out, it was going to make for one awkward weekend.

"Come on," he said, holding out his hand to help her up.

Still silent but all smiles, she grabbed his hand. Chris held a robe out for her and led her past the glass doors and outside to the patio. Klara's knees were still shaking enough that she had to grip Chris's hand hard so as not to fall over. She was still in disbelief that she was in Christopher Kaiser's house, that she'd just sucked Christopher Kaiser off, and that Christopher Kaiser was actually falling for her. She could totally see it in his eyes, in the way he looked at her when he thought she wasn't paying attention. She did the same to him.

Does he know, too, then? That I'm in love? At least, she was pretty damn sure she was in love.

"What would you like to drink? Water? Coffee? Champagne?" he offered.

"Champagne? It's the middle of the day!"

"Oh, you can't tell me you haven't ever tried day-drinking before!"

"I don't know where you would ever get that idea! I'm totally innocent," she said playfully.

"Champagne it is then, dahling!"

Klara's eyes followed him as he crossed the patio and disappeared through a different door.

Is there anything Chris can't do? Anything Chris doesn't have? The house. The career. The charisma. The bedroom skills. The sense of humor that almost … almost rivals my own. He was amazing, and she planned on telling him just how amazing he was. After she had a few drinks. *Maybe.*

"Bubbly for the princess!" he said, handing her a shiny glass of liquid gold and holding his own up for her, waiting. "I want to toast to you, Klara."

"Me? For what?"

"You've grown leaps and bounds just in this short week I've known you. You gave up the strict schedules, and now, look at you. You're on a beach, sipping champagne, in the middle of the day, and you're nearing the halfway mark in your novel. I'm damn impressed."

Klara blushed. She was never one to be the best at receiving compliments. Not these types of compliments. Sure, people would tell her they liked her dress, her perfume, or her whatever it was that was just practical. Never had anyone said they were impressed by her. Never.

"It's all you, Chris. You have been an amazing instructor. Not only that, but you've also been my muse. I've learned a lot this week. In all the ways."

Limerence.

He was going to have to tell her. He knew she was falling, and he wanted to let her know it was okay. It wasn't the big, scary L-word. It couldn't be. They hadn't even known each other long. He wanted to make her his. The limerence, like a drug. She was a drug. He didn't want to stop.

Can we really do this? Would she even want to?

He poured them more champagne, took a big gulp, and let it all out. "Klara?"

"Yeah?" she said, looking at him like something was wrong. She knew this face, she knew that quiet voice, she knew that familiar dread settling in around her.

"I have so enjoyed this week with you. A lot. Probably more than is acceptable and maybe borderline creepy."

"I have, too, and I feel the same. You're good for me. Every bit of me."

"Yes, you're my muse as well. You've sparked my mind. You've sparked my body. You've sparked my soul."

This was going a lot better than Klara had thought it would. Maybe he was about to say the L-word.

Oh, she hoped he was, so she could breathe a sigh of relief. *Should I say it back? Should I wait? Should I say I thought I loved him, too? Is it the day-drinking getting to me? Is this even real?*

"Thank you, Chris. That's very sweet of you to say. You've definitely set me ablaze as well."

"I think there is a better name for what we have. It's like chemistry but better. Have you heard of limerence?"

What the fuck? Klara's voice caught in her throat. "I know what limerence is." *It's not fucking love; that's what it is.*

"I think that is what I'm feeling. I'm crazy about you. Do you feel it, too?"

"Yes," she lied. No, it wasn't limerence for her. She really did love Chris, but now, she knew where he stood on those feelings for her. She had been so silly, believing, wishing, dreaming that all of this could work. That all of this was anything other than limerence. *What bullshit.*

"I was hoping we could continue down this path, embrace it, and see where it goes."

And, now, he was feeding her hope. Limerence and hope.

Do I really have time for this?

He could probably read the emotions on her face, but she had enough champagne to not care anymore.

"What do you mean, continue down this path? See where it goes?"

"I mean, I don't want to give you up next week. I want to keep this up. You're good for me, and you just said I was good for you, too. I think we should date. Keep in touch and all. I'm completely obsessed, infatuated, and limerence-stricken with you."

Klara didn't know why he kept repeating that word. *Is he trying to reassure himself? Or is he trying to reassure me?*

"I don't know how this would work long-distance, Chris. I mean, how often would we really be able to see each other?"

"I can swing by to spend some days in between travels, and you can always, always come here. If things are going really well for us, we can work it out," he said, putting down his glass. "What do you say?"

She bit her lip, unable to think from a combination of his gorgeous body crawling on top of her and the champagne bubbles tingling her brain.

"Are you asking me to date you exclusively, as in become a couple, or am I just a side piece for your fun between travels?"

"You really are stubborn, aren't you? I don't want you giving up on Farmer John, but yes, I would love to date you properly. Now, I know it will be tough, being in another state, but maybe it will give us just the right amount of coupledom while we can still focus on career choices. How does that sound?"

"Well, if we are to become a couple, we'll have to come up with one of those couple names," Klara said, melting into him.

His body on top of her, he quickly undid the ties of her robe and his. This was what she wanted. She wanted to be with him. She loved him. Not this limerence bullshit. Real love. She knew it because she wanted him to be happy even if it broke her heart.

"Klaris? Chrisara? The unstoppable duo?" he teased in between kissing her.

"Those are terrible."

"Yeah, we have time to come up with it. All the time."

"Let's do it," she agreed.

If it wasn't love now, maybe, with more time, it would be for him. He was good for her. If anything, he was right about long-distance leaving them time to fulfill their own goals. She could use this whirlwind romance to make progress in her own life even if it tore her apart in the end. It would be worth it. He would be worth it. He'd better be worth it.

Chris didn't know if it was the sea breeze, the champagne, or Klara that was making him crazy. Probably a combo of all three. But, damn, he was in a state of bliss. He had a beautiful woman in his house, a woman who had all the giddy emotions for him as he did her. A smart woman. A funny woman. A kind woman. An extraordinary blow-your-socks-off kind of woman. A woman he could count on to stand by him, and he'd do the same for her.

A muse. A wife.

Wait, what? Limerence. Limerence. Limerence.

SEVEN

Chris's parents were out of the country on vacation and needed his help with tying up some loose ends around the now-extinct family business. Even when the work stopped, it never stopped with his dad. The man was every bit of a business professional. Always dressed in a suit and tie, always extremely proper, almost military-like in his demeanor. He could sell a bucket of fire to clients roasting in hell. His brain and his work never stopped. Not even after retirement. His mom, much the same. But Chris? Chris hadn't inherited the corporate gene. Much to his parents' dismay, he would rather have his head in a book than in a conference call.

But that didn't stop Chris from being dragged into some of the family investments, which he was extremely grateful for. Writing hadn't exactly paid the bills up until recently. He was fortunate to have, well, a fortune. So, when his parents had called and needed his help, he was more than happy to give it to them. They'd steered him in the right direction in life even if they didn't fully support the path he ultimately chose. Besides, he had Marcy supporting his goals, and she had been around much more often than his parents.

Marcy … shit! he thought.

He had forgotten that Marcy had a key to his house, and sometimes, she used it on the weekends to "cure writer's block" when she knew he would be away. Chris hadn't even thought about Marcy. He was too busy thinking about the feel of Klara's nipples under his fingertips, the sexy little freckle right where her right thigh met her hip bone. His morning had been completely consumed with thoughts of her.

Chris checked his watch. He had been in his dad's office all morning, cleaning up old business accounts, handling documents, and organizing financials for their investments. Maybe Marcy wouldn't show up this weekend. But, with his luck, he thought he should call to check in and casually mention he would be in town this weekend.

"Marcy, hey! How are you?"

"Chris! I'm doing good. Really good now that I've met your girlfriend."

"My what?"

"Klara! And let me tell you, Chris, she is a *doll!* We've been trading stories back and forth this morning. Enjoying some girl time by the waves."

Chris's voice stuttered, "What kind of stories?"

"Oh, you know. The kind that embarrass you. Like the time you pooped the tub as a baby, the time you passed out during the school play, the time you—"

"Marcy!" Chris was already in his car and on his way home by the time she'd said she was trading stories.

"I'm kidding! I'm kidding! Chris, it's just me here right now. Klara went in to get us some snacks. Thank the good Lord I'd stocked your fridge! She looks as tiny as a toothpick. She needs a bagel or something! Take her out somewhere fancy tonight. Feed that poor child!"

"She's not starving, and damn, don't scare me like that! I'm not trying to have her running for the hills."

"What's that mean? You like her? Really, really like her? Didn't you two just meet up in Memphis? She did say y'all discussed dating long-distance, but she didn't mention anything else about it after that."

"She did?" Chris was curious.

He guessed he could be an adult and just ask, but what if that was a bad idea? *What if she has no hope for long-distance?* He kind of thought that was the truth anyway. He'd sensed her caution when he mentioned making it work. He at least *thought* he could make it work. *I'll do my best to make it work, damn it.* He wasn't ready to come down off this ride yet. He already had plans to write about their experiences in his next book. Not everything, of course. He'd like some of their secrets to remain his.

"Don't go breaking her heart, Chris. If you got a career to chase, you'd better let her know. She seems really nice. Don't love her and leave her like all the other girls in all the other cities."

"Well, that's not fair. I never really cared this much about any of them. Besides, they were different. They weren't ... " Chris stammered. "They weren't Klara. There's something about her. I just feel like she's special. I don't want to mess it up. I'm trying to make it work. That means, slow down on my scheduling, please. I'll be needing as many stops in Memphis as I can make."

Marcy was happy for Chris. She'd wondered if he would ever actually put in any effort into dating a woman instead of just frolicking around with them on his trips. *Maybe he is scared? Maybe he is just too busy with his career?* Whatever it was, he wasn't a spring chicken anymore, and she worried about his future and how much longer he could be alone.

"Of course she's special. She probably has more brains in her pinkie than those other women had in their heads. Put together! She's also quite the character. She had me laughing until I almost wet myself, telling me about how y'all met and you playing Mr. Hero. Really, I wouldn't expect less from you. You're special, too, you know. You deserve to be happy, Chris. And loved."

"I didn't say I was in love. No one said anything about love! I just met her. It's just limerence."

"Limer-what? What's that mean?" Marcy was baffled. She'd never heard the word before, but a feeling of dread had come over her as soon as he said it.

"It's like love but without the love part. That might complicate things," Chris explained.

"Oh, honey. Really? Does she know you feel this way?"

"Told her yesterday when we decided to keep this going," Chris answered happily. Proud of himself for stating his feelings.

"Do me a favor. If you ever mention an L-word again, to any woman, you'd better mean it, and it'd better not be this limerence hullabaloo."

"Why is that a bad thing?" The blood drained from Chris's face as he started to second-guess himself.

"You think a woman wants to be told, *I limerence you,* or that you basically aren't comfortable enough with her, or yourself, to let yourself love her. Like there's something wrong with either or both of you?"

Marcy was losing patience. *Is Chris really this dense in love?* She needed to have a long talk with him.

"So, you're saying I shouldn't have told her? Because it's the truth; it's how I feel."

"Have you been in love before, Chris?"

"No. Never."

"Then, how do you know that's not how you feel? Maybe what you're trying to label as limerence is really love."

Chris thought about what she'd said. *How would I even know what love is like? I wouldn't.*

"I don't want to complicate things. You know, in case it doesn't work out long-distance. Besides, we still don't even know each other much. She could be a felon or a secret society witch. Who knows?"

"You know, I believe you know exactly how you feel. And, when you love someone, you make it work. No matter what. So, if that happens, if you do quit the limerence horseshit and come to your senses and let yourself feel something ... more ... then you'd better be sure before you commit. Because I see the look in her eyes when she talks about you. That's not limerence."

"You do? What kind of look?" Chris had a lump in his throat.

"She's coming back out. I've gotta go! I'm assuming you're coming back, so I'll see you soon."

Marcy hung up before he got to ask more questions. He wondered if he'd hurt Klara's feelings yesterday.

Maybe I should have just kept my mouth shut. Maybe I shouldn't have told her how I felt. I just thought she felt the same, and maybe it would help her internal struggle, too. But does she even have an internal struggle? Am I projecting? He needed to stop reading *Psychology Today*, or maybe he should read it more. It helped with his novels' characters, but he guessed it could benefit him, too.

By the time he pulled into his driveway and made his way out back, Klara and Marcy had already set him up a beach chair.

"Look who decided to step away from the office!" Marcy said as she passed him a beer.

"Yeah, well, we can't all live the glamorous life of spending our days on the beach, day-drinking."

"Says who?" Klara teased.

Her hair was pulled back in her infamous sexy bun. Wisps of curls danced in the wind, framing her face. Chris noticed how happy she was here. He could watch her smile like this all day long.

"Hear, hear!" Marcy held up her beer in response to Klara.

"I see you've met Marcy. Marcy, Klara. Klara, Marcy," Chris said, making the proper introductions lest Klara think he was some type of rude jerk.

"We know; we know. We've been best friends for, oh, about six hours now. Come sit." Marcy motioned to the empty beach chair.

He could tell the two ladies were well on their way to Drunk Town. Klara, who he had seen only tipsy at the hotel, was flushed, as if she had just stepped off his ride. Her cheeks blushing, her lips parted. Marcy, on the other hand, was sweating like a hog roasting over a firepit. Her head rolled back, and her feet dug into the sand. She was already in Drunk Town. She was the mayor of Drunk Town.

What have I gotten myself into now?

"Did you know that Marcy here told me about your gator?" Klara asked, eyeing Chris and suppressing her giggles.

"My what?"

"Your gator, Chris! You know, Tom?"

"Oh, sheesh, Marcy. Yes, I had a stuffed gator named Tom, growing up. Still have him actually."

"In your nightstand," Klara finished.

"To be fair, Marcy put him in there. But he does warm up my lonely nights."

"Ha!" Marcy chimed in. "Lonely? Chris could wink and have any woman within a fifty-mile radius here."

Okay, now, she was really drunk. Chris prepared himself to do damage control.

"But he doesn't," she continued, winking at him. "Chris is a gentleman. And, if going back to school has taught me anything at my old age, it's that there isn't a lot of them left. I'd say you found yourself a good one."

"Hear, hear!" Klara echoed, grinning from ear to ear. "But I think he found me."

"Touché," Marcy toasted. Her beer held in the air, arm swaying like it weighed ten pounds.

"So glad I did. And I'm so glad I saved you from that farming life with Farmer John. You know how hard farming is on the body?" Chris said, throwing back his beer and letting himself join in on the party.

Klara and Chris bantered back and forth on how the story went, not noticing that Marcy had nodded off until they heard what sounded like a constipated dinosaur. The noise jarred them both as they looked over at Marcy's head, lying back, her mouth open, eyes closed. Her snores were startling and downright terrifying.

"Is she ... is she okay?" Klara worried about the older lady. She had never heard such noises before. There was snoring, and then there was this, whatever it was that Marcy was doing. Summoning a mythical creature from the dead? Regurgitating a human hair ball? Was she in pain? Did she need help? An exorcism?

Chris couldn't help but laugh. "Nope, this is just Marcy. She could wake the dead, I know!"

He got up and gently nudged her, helping her to her feet. "Wakey-wakey! Let's go get you down for a nap, Granny!"

"Granny!" Marcy muttered. "I'll show you a gran—" But then she decided to just stop right there. She was way too old and way too drunk to keep going. She took Chris's arm as he led her back inside.

"Back for a swim in just a minute!" Chris nodded at Klara.

It wasn't the first time he had helped Marcy, but then again, she had done it for him plenty of times, too.

"Can I help?" Klara offered, her expression still worried.

Chris shook his head and continued on into the house. He led Marcy to the guest room and set her up on the bed. Plumping her pillow, getting her a glass of water, and making sure she was comfortable before he left. She had already fallen asleep before he turned to go.

Chris grinned mischievously. Now, he had Klara all to himself.

The sand was scorching hot on his feet as he ran frantically down the beach, passing Klara, and he jumped right into the waves. Hollering like he had just won the lottery because, in a way, he had. Klara laughed at his antics as he motioned for her to join. She stood up, untied her robe, and dramatically let it fall to the ground. Chris stood as still as a statue. His eyes lingering, his mouth watering. Klara knew she was teasing him. She'd brought her most erotic bikini just for this moment. Something she'd bought in one of her rabbit-hole late-night internet adventures but not yet dared to wear anywhere.

The black string bikini barely covered any of her. It was about as good as putting on two pasties over her nipples and a Band-Aid over her slit. But it did the trick, obviously, because Chris looked about two seconds from drowning if he didn't snap out of it and watch the waves that were getting rougher and rougher. She slowly sauntered over to him, looking up and down the beach to make sure no one was around. Klara unhooked her top and cast it aside. She giggled as she heard Chris gasp over the sound of the ocean.

"You'd better be coming over here to put those lips on me! I need those lips on me. Let me taste the salt on your neck," he called to her as she entered the warm water and made her way to him.

He slipped his hands under her bottom and held her tight as she wrapped her arms and legs around him. They both bobbed up and down with each wave. His cock stiff against her. Their tongues exploring each other's mouths.

He pulled back to look at her. "You're so damn beautiful, Klara. Do you know that? You aren't even of this world. You're so fucking gorgeous, and I'm so fucking lucky," he said as he roughly kissed her.

Klara's nipples hardened against his chest as the bobbing waves rubbed his cock against her clit. She sighed into his mouth as she rolled her hips back and forth, rubbing herself against his swollen cock.

"You're so damn good. So damn good," she muttered, her breaths starting to stutter.

He sensed she was getting close to orgasm, and he hadn't even done anything. The fact that she was getting off from just grinding against him made him even more turned on. He grabbed her by the hips and moved her quickly up and down the length of his cock, making her gasp. He could feel her legs twitching as they wrapped tightly around his back.

"Fuck. Oh, fuck yes. Chris, I'm … I'm … "

He pulled her in harder, faster. Both of them were breathing heavily, still bobbing and splashing in the waves.

"Kiss me when you do. I want your lips on mine the second you come."

Klara nodded her head, barely able to think enough to even lift her head. She could feel her pulse running through her feet, and that was when she knew she was about to lose all control.

"Ahh—" she cried out.

As soon as he could, he put his mouth on hers, muffling her gasps, while he still rocked her back and forth against him. Her hands twitched. Her feet twitched. Her legs twitched. Her hips were pulled in tight against him as she hung on to him like he was a lifesaver.

Klara slowly kissed him, her eyes still closed in a state of ecstasy.

"Come on. Let's go inside and get you taken care of," she whispered into his mouth. She would do anything for Chris right now. She was putty in his hands.

"Get me taken care of? I have all the time in the world for that! My pleasure is your pleasure. I think I want to stay here a little longer, holding you. I'm putting this one in my memory bank."

Klara was putting their rendezvous in her memory bank, too. She had never done anything like that before. In the middle of the ocean, in public—again. Thankfully, the beach was secluded. She guessed not many people walked down to the far end where his house sat, which was a good thing because she could get used to hot, public-beach sex with Chris.

Damn it, Chris. Why do you have to be so damn perfect? Except for that whole emotionally-unavailable thing with the limerence and all.

She wondered if his caution had anything to do with the way his parents hadn't been around much. Marcy had alluded to the fact, but she never confirmed anything.

Poor Chris, she thought. *He deserves all the love. Fuck this limerence bullshit.*

Klara shivered.

"You cold?"

"Just a little," Klara lied.

She wanted to tell him the truth. She wanted to tell him that she was a big dumb-dumb and believed in love at first sight. At least, she did now that she was looking at him. But, instead, she let it go. She didn't want to be *that* crazy woman and scare away a good thing. His rejection was the last thing she needed.

"Come on; let's go inside, take a hot bath, order some pizza, and get some writing done before bed. Plane leaves around two tomorrow, so we won't need to be up too early. I'll make you breakfast." He smiled.

I mean, come on. Can this man get any more perfect? Klara mused.

"Well, damn, you sure do know the way to my heart. That sounds perfect." And she said it. She said the word *heart*, and she put it out there. She wanted to cover it with flowers and big flashing signs, throw some glitter on that shit, and make it sing. Maybe then he would understand how she felt.

Chris wondered if she'd meant that. He got the impression that the way to her heart was through her perfectly organized calendar, whispering dirty and filthy things into her ears, six-pack abs, and cocktails. *Can she really be as easy as pizza and a night in?* He was deep in his thoughts when he realized what she'd really said was that he knew her heart. That international symbol of love.

Is she hinting at her feelings? Or does she really just want to crash and be lazy tonight? Or maybe she wants to go party but doesn't want to make me feel bad for my lame suggestion of staying in?

Nah, that wasn't her. He knew. He had seen it in her eyes when he came home from work today. The way she looked up at him, even as he was disheveled in his button-down and trousers. Sweating like he had in the humid heat back in Memphis. She was deep in the limerence feels, too. It couldn't be love. She was way too smart for that. Klara was going places, and he didn't want to mess that up for her.

But …

He shook the thoughts from his head. *Love.* He wasn't sure he had ever loved. He never stayed still long enough to let that happen. He'd had deep feelings for some of his flings, but they never lasted. He never let them. Sure, he wrote about love plenty. But that all came from the books he'd read. Not from experience. The sex, well, yeah, that was totally from experience. He had no trouble with that. But the icky, sticky, gooey, gushy stuff? No clue about it.

He ran the bath for them both, drowning out Marcy's snores all the way from the other side of the house. He didn't know how she did it. She must have four lungs. The poor lady. He wondered how her husband had slept with her when he was alive. He'd died ages ago, when Chris was very young. He didn't remember much about the man, except that he always had a piece of candy in his pocket. It was those almost-metal-like hard candies that old people liked, but it was still candy, so Chris never turned it down. Besides, it would last him all day.

"Does she stay here often?" Klara said as Chris helped her into the warm bath.

"Who? Marcy? Not too often. Usually only when I'm gone on the weekends. I just forgot to tell her I was coming this weekend. Last minute and all."

"She seems lonely."

"Really? Why would you say that? Did she tell you she was?"

Klara picked up on the worry in Chris's voice.

"No, not exactly. She talked about her kids being all grown up and having their own lives these days. She said she still sees them at school, but she thinks they avoid her, being the old lady on campus and all. She also talked about her late husband for a while. She really loved him. What they had sounded ... special."

"I don't remember him much. She's never even mentioned him much to me. I always thought it made her too sad to talk about him, so I didn't push on questions. I'm surprised she opened up to you," Chris said, grabbing Klara's foot and massaging it.

Klara groaned and sank deeper into the warm water. Chris had magic hands. Anytime he touched her, she melted.

"I don't think she is sad about it. I think she wanted to talk about it. He seemed like he was her soul mate. Like a twin flame, she said. Have you heard of that? The book she is working on is about twin flames."

"Yeah, I know what a twin flame is. Do you believe in all that? Soul mates? Twin flames? True love? Love at first sight?"

"The princess in me would say, hell yes. I can belt out every Disney song like any other fangirl. Someday, my prince will come and blah, blah. But my head says ... or said ... no. So, I guess I don't know."

Chris caught the past tense. He noticed her eyes staring into the water. She wouldn't look up at him as she kept talking. His thoughts were lost in her voice.

"What about you? Ever been in love?"

Chris suddenly grew even hotter. This was a conversation he wasn't sure how to get out of. If he told her the truth, that he had never loved, she would surely think something was wrong with him. At his age and never been in love? He might as well tell her he had a hidden collection of Ronald McDonald paraphernalia or a fetish for dirty socks. That would send her away just as fast as having commitment issues.

"I—"

She waited in an awkward silence. Prompting him to continue. She had him trapped in the bathtub.

Time to open up, buddy.

If she could give him her body, herself, her heart, he could give her what was going on in his mind.

"I haven't had the chance to be in love. Now, I know that sounds bad. An old guy like me. But I'm just being honest with you. I've been too busy with my career, and I've never sat still long enough to find the one. Or a one. Or someone." Chris shrugged. This time, it was his eyes averting hers.

"So, if it hit you right in the face, you wouldn't even know what it was?"

"I guess not. I've never really thought about it. I mean, I guess my parents love each other, but they weren't ever really around either to show me how that looks. Man, I'd better stop now. I sound like a walking *Psychology Manual* or a *Huffington Post* article on who not to hook up with."

Klara laughed. She was so glad he was opening up to her.

"Well, you sure do write some good love stories for someone who has never been in love."

"I read a lot," he said, which was true.

"Well, that's not real love. That's fairy-tale love. Now, I know that shit isn't real. Love takes work. It takes a choice to commit to someone. Day after day, night after night. Sometimes, it hurts."

"Hurts? How?"

"Because, when you love someone, you want them to be happy. No matter what. No matter what that means for you. Even if it means you aren't in the picture anymore. That's how you know it's love."

They both sat in awkward silence. The water growing cooler, their words hanging in the air. All this talk of love, and the familiar sadness was back again. For Klara, it was because she had hoped this conversation would go a different way. For Chris, it was because he felt like a huge failure in life, and he was ashamed for Klara to know it.

"How do you know all this? Did you have someone you loved?" he said, cutting through the tense air like a hot knife.

"Are you kidding me? I dated a bunch of Farmer Asshats! I just read a lot, too. Maybe too many self-help books. So, there. Now, we are even on the field of shame."

Chris laughed as Klara lifted the mood with her always-witty remarks. If he did love someone, it would be someone like her. Or her. He didn't know anymore. The limerence was getting to him.

"I feel like this conversation is just too damn deep to have sober. I think I need to do something manly. Like throw some axes or do a keg stand."

"Manly? Now, don't tell me you are all about toxic masculinity and that alpha-male bullshit and that you can't talk about your feelings."

Shit. He knew better than to say something like that. Even if it wasn't what he meant. But he did totally mean it. Talking about his feelings made him super uncomfortable. He was going to have to work on that. For Klara.

"You're right! I'm so uncomfortable, talking about my feelings! I feel like I need to yell like Tarzan or something. Help!"

"Did you say I was right?"

"Yes."

"You're so fucking perfect," she growled.

"Except for the fact that I just perpetuated alpha-male culture and played into the stereotype when you're working hard to smash the patriarchy."

"Dude, you said I was right. That's a damn good step in the right direction. Now, get out of this tub and fuck me like an animal. You can do your Tarzan yell then."

Chris looked at Klara as if she had two heads. *Did she really just say that?* He was so turned on by the look in her eyes. Her pupils dilated, as she was ready to devour him. *Who knew telling a woman she was right would make her go primal?* He was going to file this one in his memory bank, too.

Klara stood up, biting her lip, her fists clenched as she held herself back. Chris pulled the drain, stood up, and looked her square in the eyes.

"You, Klara." He pointed toward her. "Me, Chris." He pointed toward himself. He beat his chest with his fists, swept her off her feet, and carried her to bed.

EIGHT

"Ouch! Memphis heat!" Chris groaned as they stepped off the plane. "How do you even survive these summers?"

"Copious amounts of alcohol and air-conditioning." Klara smiled.

She was used to the sticky mess that seemed to last more than half the year. She thought it had to be better than having a freezing cold winter. She wasn't a cold-weather type person. At all. She needed to be out and about with her hands in the dirt and a warm breeze in her hair. She sighed, already missing the beach. Chris was so damn lucky to call it his home.

"Alcohol and air-conditioning. Right. Good plan. Want to get some writing done in the lobby with some drinks?"

"Actually, I was thinking I needed to swing by Miss May's and check on her. I'm usually over there just about every other day. I need to make sure she's watering those plants! I can swing by later though?" Klara answered him without any bit of hesitation.

"Uh, okay. Sure. Sounds good."

Chris was a little confused. *Am I imagining things, or is she being short with me?* He wouldn't mind seeing Miss May either, but he got the feeling he shouldn't invite himself. He went through the day's events in his head to see if anything he had done would have pissed her off. He had nothing. The day had been a great one. Breakfast in bed, sex, shower, more sex, flirting at the airport, contemplating sex on the plane and ultimately both chickening out, silly conversations, a lot of laughter, and now, they were here. Distant. Almost. Or she was at least.

"I want to thank you, Chris, for inviting me to your home. For taking me on an amazing trip. For helping me with my work. For listening to my babbling. And for just being such a good friend."

Friend, he thought. *So, she is distancing herself.*

"Klara, you're worth every bit of it and more. You've helped me with my work too, ya know. I've not been able to write nonstop like this in a very, very long time. You've given me so much motivation."

"The feeling is mutual. I think I'll be done with my book by the end of the summer. And I already have two more planned. That's all you."

"Not a chance, Klara. That is all *you*. I've just been lucky enough to point you in the right direction. But you've been heading that way all along."

Klara sighed and gave him a peck on the lips. She was now back in reality, and there were five more sleeps until she had to say good-bye for who knew how long. *How am I ever going to do this long-distance thing?* She was going to have to check Amazon's self-help section on this type of relationship. She imagined lots and lots of phone sex in her future.

They drove in silence, ignoring the familiar sadness wrapped around them. Her shoulders slumped as she tuned the radio to something, anything, that wasn't going to make her ugly cry. Classical. He liked classical. She was okay with classical. Klara let her mind drift as the music took over. Her mood seemed to be lifting with the high notes, the violin playing a chipper beat. Klara was dancing inside to the beat of the symphony when her stomach rudely began to join the concert.

"What the fuck was that? Was that … was that your stomach?"

Klara hadn't eaten since breakfast, and she hadn't even realized she was hungry until she smelled the familiar scent of barbecue hanging in the air downtown. When she recognized the bubbling in her stomach, the one that came as a warning sign that her bowels were about to shake her whole body in frustration unless she fed them now, it was too late to panic.

"I think I might be just a bit hungry," Klara said, mortified. Her face turning bright red.

How can I be embarrassed of my stomach growling? Really? Am I ten?

This man had seen her spread-eagle on the bed. Facedown, ass up. Balloon knot and all. But her stomach did sound dangerous at the moment. Like it was going to crawl out of her mouth and kick Chris in the face if he kept on going. Hangry. She was about to be hangry.

"Jeez Louise! That sounded angry! Are you drowning some cats in your stomach acid in there? Pull over, and let's get you something to eat! That can't be good, Klara! I think you're eating yourself from the inside out."

Klara laughed, noticing the mood in the car now had done a complete one-eighty. No more sadness, just laughter and rabid growling from her stomach. At least her focus was now on how to shut her stomach up and not on how to keep herself from crying in front of Chris. *Oh, the horror!* That would be much worse, much, much worse. She was glad her insatiable appetite had intervened.

"I'm okay! I'll get something quick at home before I head back out. I'm going to shower and all. You know, airports are icky!" Her stomach growled again, as if responding to her.

"Okay, but I'm outta here before it eats me up!" he said as they pulled into the hotel drop-off. He dramatically hopped out of the car, grabbed his bag, and ran for his life back inside with his hands waving around like a maniac.

Klara laughed hysterically at his antics before pulling away. The doorman shook his head like he had already seen enough for today.

Now that she was alone—and in a much better mood, thanks to her rumbly tummy—Klara finally had a chance to think and take in all that had happened during the weekend. She had to tell someone. And, while her acquaintances from school couldn't know about the naughty visiting author, she knew Ms. May would be more than glad to lend her an ear. Klara put on her love-songs playlist, turned it up, and sang her heart out as she drove. Cloud nine wasn't even good enough. Klara was on cloud fifty-three and a half. The half being the tiny little part in her brain that told her it would soon be time for him to go. But she quieted that part with cheesy lyrics and terrible tone.

When she pulled up to Ms. May's house, the street was eerily quiet for a late Sunday. She knew Ms. May would be cooking Sunday supper around this time. Her house would smell of roast, bacon fat, butter. But there wasn't any scent of food in the air as she stepped on the porch to ring the bell. She waited but no answer. Klara paced the porch, noticing the rose bushes were looking parched. She decided to grab the hose and water them as she waited. Maybe Ms. May was in the back or on the toilet. She knew how old people were slow. She had patience.

"Klara?" she heard a voice calling from the porch next door.

It was Ms. May's neighbor, Gloria. Gloria was everything Ms. May was not. Kind, sweet, gentle, and a walking Bible. She could quote a scripture for every situation.

"Gloria! How are you? I was just looking for Ms. May. Have you seen her?"

"Oh, I'm so sorry, sugar. She's at the hospital," Gloria answered sorrowfully.

"The hospital?" Klara started to panic. *I was gone two days, and that old bag decides to pull this crap?* "What for? Is she all right?"

"Nobody knows. She left in the middle of the night. Been gone since Friday when the ambulance picked her up. But we have faith that she's okay. She's a tough one. *The Lord nurses them when they are sick and restores them to health.* Psalm 41:3."

"Which hospital, Gloria? I'll head there now to check on her."

"Central, I'm sure. It's the only one they take us to around here," Gloria said, her voice flat.

She and Ms. May had lived next door to each other over half of their lives, and even though they didn't always get along, Gloria had a soft spot for Ms. May. She was just another soul that needed saving after all.

Klara started to sweat and shake as she made her way to Central Hospital. Her foot heavy on the gas pedal. *What if Ms. May is gone? What if she is dead? What if she is in a coma? What if she just broke a toe and wanted to be dramatic?* The last sounded most plausible, but Klara braced herself for the worst when she walked through those glass doors. The place smelled like chemicals, mixed with meds, mixed with death. She knew she wouldn't last very long in here. Klara could never work in a medical environment. Her stomach was queasy just from the smell alone. Her appetite suddenly gone.

"I'm looking for my friend. Marilyn May. She was brought in Friday."

"Down the hall, to the left, room 121," the nurse at the desk answered without looking up from her phone.

Thank God she's not dead at least, Klara thought, making her way down the brightly lit hallway.

Her eyes scanned the room numbers, searching for Ms. May's room, but she soon found out she didn't need to do that. She saw a nurse step out of a room and throw her hands up in the air, defeated. That was the room Ms. May had to be in.

"Knock, knock!" She tapped on the door.

"Come in. I know who it is. I heard your goofy gait click-clacking down the hall. It's 'bout damn time. You gonna tell me where the hell you been? Because the only excuse good enough for you not coming to check on me earlier would be you being laid up in here, next to me."

Klara pushed the door open, took one look at the weak woman in the bed, and caught her breath. She had been prepared to say something snarky back but held off, terrified of what was happening to her old friend.

"You look terrible, Ms. May! What the hell happened?"

"You don't look like a spring chicken either, young lady. Now, where you been?"

"You first! What's going on? What's all this for?" Klara said, motioning to the monitors, the IVs, the meds.

"Heart attack. I almost died. I saw my life flash before my eyes, Klara. And it was a bad one! So bad! I need to get my ass back in church because that light was turning dark. So dark."

"You were probably passing out; that's why!"

"Look here, Ms. Know-It-All! I know what I seen. And Ms. May has some explaining to do one of these days."

"You can start here and now. Explain to me. Are you okay? Do you hurt? When do you go home? What can I do to help you?" Klara questioned her old friend. Her voice quivered with fear and concern.

"Yes, yes, and sometime this week, they best be letting me. If I have to eat one more piece of this old folks' mush, I told that nurse she's gonna find this bedpan flying across the room!"

"Well, that isn't very nice! Remember that light turning dark? I think being nice to your nurse is a step in the right direction to getting in God's good graces now, don't you?"

Ms. May rolled her eyes, crossed her arms, and pursed her lips.

"Your turn. Why you leave me when I was at my weakest point? You just upped and disappeared last week. I didn't know if you was murdered, sick, fired, or what!"

"I was with him. Chris," Klara whispered, trying to hold back a smile. Because smiling in this place, with that poor old coot laid up like that, well, that wouldn't be right. At least, Klara thought so.

But, when she looked up at Ms. May, Ms. May was beaming.

"Uh-huh. So, Chris. Tell me, when y'all having babies?"

"I'm not even married yet!"

"Girl, I told you, men are trouble. You don't need to be marrying 'em to get the goods."

"But what if I want to marry them? Him? Someone? Eventually. After school and all." Klara's voice trailed off.

"Does he know this?"

Klara caught the sparkle in Ms. May's eye.

"Know what?"

"Don't play dumb with me, Klara. Does he know you love him?" Ms. May's eyes were narrowed, as she was clearly trying to read Klara's mind.

"I don't love him! I only just met him."

"You do," Ms. May muttered, not skipping a beat.

"I don't!"

"You do."

"No, I don't! Besides, he just limerences me," Klara said, rolling her eyes.

"He what?"

"Limerence. It's like being in love but not being in love. He said it's natural to feel this way and that we can try dating long-distance because he really limerences me. Or something like that. So, I'm just going to limerence him back."

"I'm going to limerence my foot in his ass the next time I see him."

"Remember the darkness, Ms. May."

"He's gonna see the darkness. What kind of shit is that? Limerence. Klara, you'd better not go any further; you are gonna get hurt. He clearly ain't the committing type, just like all of them. *All* of them," Ms. May urged her, shaking her head in disgust.

"I'm trying, Ms. May, but I had such a magical weekend with him, and I—"

"Magic ain't real, honey. If he's making excuses to himself and to you about how he feels, he's afraid. And most men who are afraid, they run like cowards. Limerence? I never heard no man use that line. Sounds like a bunch of bullshit to me. Like lust, just lust. And that's easier to say. Sounds to me like he just wants your goods."

"I guess he feels more than lust though. According to him."

"That would be love—or falling in love at least. He can't say that word? Run."

"It's only been a week."

"Have you been spending every day with him since y'all met?"

"Yes."

"Have y'all been going at it like rabbits every day? Looking all doe-eyed and mouthwatering like ya about to eat each other up?"

"Yes." Klara had no shame. She was still on cloud fifty-three and a half, except slowly decreasing that number with all this sense Ms. May was making.

"Do you love him?" Ms. May continued. Her head bobbing back and forth with each point she was making.

"Yes."

"See? You already know. Women know. Men know, too. They just don't admit it. They don't feel safe. Too vulnerable. Cowards."

"I'm not telling him how I feel either though! That's embarrassing! He'll think I'm crazy for falling so fast!"

"Good. Don't tell him. And back off. He ain't committing, and things are about to get real hard when he leaves."

Klara nodded. She knew Ms. May was right, and here she went down the path of what-ifs again. *What if this next week he fell in love and said it? What if they were able to make it work long-distance? What if we got married and I had his beautiful babies? I would love to have Chris's babies. What the hell is wrong with me? Does love make me crazy? Or limerence?*

He seemed more levelheaded than her. It had to just be limerence to him. Ms. May was right; she should run. But she didn't want to.

"I hear ya. And I agree. I'll try to turn my feelings off. But I still want to give it a shot."

"I'm not saying, don't give it a shot. I'm just saying, take care of yourself. Be careful. On guard. Focus on your book. How is that book coming along anyway? Am I in it? You'd better not be painting me as a crazy old bag!"

"But isn't that what you are?" Klara teased, changing the subject.

"Don't go and give me another heart attack now, child!" Ms. May wagged her finger at Klara.

Ms. May laughed and went along with the book discussion. She knew she had to stop talking about Chris and letting Klara down about the reality of her situation. *But, damn it, Klara is going to get hurt—again.* She knew Klara was making the same mistakes she had made long ago. *Always getting hurt by these men.* She couldn't talk sense into Klara. Just like no one could talk sense into her. Ms. May just kept her distance as best she could and added her snarky but sometimes wise remarks in when she could.

By the time Klara left the hospital, the sun was already starting to set. She texted Chris to let him know where she was and what had happened. He immediately called her, asking for details. She could hear the worry in his voice but assured him that it would take more than a heart hiccup to kill the devil herself.

"Do you still want to come by? I understand if you aren't feeling up for it."

Klara thought about her conversation with Ms. May and how she needed to back off. She was getting too serious with Chris. She knew it. He knew it. Everyone knew it.

"You know, I'm feeling pretty crappy. Rain check?" Klara said, hopeful he would beg her to come to the hotel.

"Yep! You got it. I'll see you in class tomorrow, okay? Let me know if you need anything, Klara. I'll be thinking about you," Chris said.

Is that disappointment in his voice? Regret? Maybe I should invite him to my house. Nah, then I would have to clean.

Klara resigned herself to getting some writing done and putting Chris out of her mind until tomorrow. At this point, she was thinking it was unhealthy, how much he ran around in her brain.

"Yep. Tomorrow. I'll be there with bells and whistles." She didn't specify what bells and whistles. She could hear funeral bells because she was pretty sure this long-distance thing was going to kill her. Though wedding bells would be nice. She wondered if she would ever hear those.

Focus on your writing. Take off your rose-colored glasses. Shape up. Ship out.

Klara was never good at positive affirmations. Who was anyway? She'd once taken a suggestion from one of her self-help books about writing positive and uplifting quotes on Post-it Notes and hanging them around the house, which she did. Except her quotes morphed from something happy to something funny to something inappropriate.

Don't shit where you eat hung on her refrigerator. *Hold my cosmo* hung on her liquor cabinet. *I'm a little bit of peace, light, and go fuck yourself* hung on her bathroom mirror. *Skeet Skeet Skeet Sleep Sleep Sleep* hung above her bed.

She'd left them up for a good part of the year until she had a short-lived fling who dropped by her house one evening, unannounced, saw the Post-its and pile of self-help books, and never called her again. She didn't care. *Who drops by, unannounced, anyway?* She wasn't the problem; he was. She obviously had her life figured out. *I mean, come on. All these self-help books and affirmations?* That just meant she was well versed in being in touch with her own feelings and worth. She would be more worried about someone who had never read a self-help book.

Her mind drifted to what kind of self-help books Chris would likely read. *How Not to Commit and Be a Playboy for Life? Love Them and Leave Them: The Gentlemen's Way? Bitches Be Crazy?*

Klara settled in for the night, pushing thoughts of Chris out of her head. Or trying to. Or at least, the bad thoughts. She knew he wasn't a bad guy. He just had commitment issues, obviously. Like most men. And she did, too. She was picky, and she knew it. She also had goals and aspirations and wasn't going to let anyone get in the way of that. Not even Chris with his swoon-worthy abs, dreamy imagination, picture-perfect face, and panty-melting, utterly filthy mouth. Nope, she had to keep levelheaded. Even if she had never been levelheaded to begin with.

Decisions, decisions, she thought, tapping her fingers across her laptop.

She was determined to finish this novel in the next few weeks. Before things got hard. Before she was a mess. Or even more of a mess than usual. She surprised herself that she had gotten this far in such a short amount of time. Where once she'd sat, scrolling through the internet for new shoes she couldn't afford, now, she was actually able to write. She had emotions, she had ideas, she had her characters well developed, and she had a muse. He sparked her fire, he sparked her brain, he sparked her body, and he sparked her soul. He was her spark. She'd never had a spark before. Not like this.

Klara checked her phone and sighed loudly. Determined. Stubborn and determined. That was what she needed to push through. Not him, not a muse. Just herself. Same as before, she only needed Klara.

She set her alarm on her phone for her usual bedtime, scribbled out *Focus, bitch* on a Post-it Note, and hung it on her desk.

NINE

Chris was on a high. Last weekend's beach rendezvous had refreshed his mind for writing and for passion. He often found himself in a trance, losing his train of thought and drifting back to the way her hair framed his face when she leaned down to kiss him. The sunlight heating up her skin, the breeze giving her chill bumps down her back, her legs, that perfect round ass of hers.

She was definitely inspiring all the hot and nasty scenes in his book, and he had a feeling she felt the same. Even if she had slightly pulled away this week. He knew she was worried about Ms. May. That was it. *Or is it?* It was already Wednesday, and she hadn't been back to the hotel. They met up for their usual coffee and writing dates after class, but the nooky had slowed way down. He didn't want to push it. He knew she was in another place right now with all she had going on. He could wait. He would be there for her. She was so damn worth it to him.

He was mesmerized by Klara. Her in all her glorious quirkiness. Bobbing her head to some one-hit wonder from the '90s while she typed away on her laptop in front of him. Damn, he was lucky. She was beautiful. And she was his. He could feel his cock thicken as she looked up to catch his eye and smile. He needed her. He wanted to show her how much he needed her. His eyes drifted down to her smile as she slowly licked her lips.

Tease, he mouthed and shook his head.

He was going to make her melt tonight. Chris had been wanting a real date night with Klara ever since they met. Somehow, things always got out of control before they made it out the door.

That usually resulted in most of their time being spent in bed or at the coffee shop. Not really dating. Not much romance.

Chris had plans. He actually wanted to spend quality time with Klara. Wining and dining her. She was a never-ending supply of fascination for him. Everything about her had sparked his interest. From the way her Southern accent disappeared when she met a stranger to the way it came on strong when she'd had one too many drinks. From the way she mentioned her mom with a quick nose flare to the way she looked far off and empty when she mentioned her dad. He wanted to know everything. However, he knew, if she let herself go to him, he would have to do the same. He wasn't quite sure how to do that.

Let myself go? Bare my heart and soul? Chris shivered.

He didn't want to come out and tell her he didn't know how to have a real relationship. How to love or even what love was. It was obvious anyway. At his age and still not committed and never able to keep a steady thing going? Nope. He probably came off as someone to avoid at all costs. He screamed commitment issues; he knew it. How was he supposed to know what love looked like? His parents loved each other; he knew that for certain. But they loved their work. Their passion was for their work. He saw their commitment to their work. They were just roommates. Supportive and positive roommates, but roommates nonetheless.

He wondered what Klara's story was. She didn't talk about her parents much. In fact, he got the gist she avoided the topic. *Is she as fucked up as I am?* He was so damn ashamed of himself. Klara was good. Too good. She didn't deserve someone who couldn't commit, no matter that he wanted to. For her, anything. He wanted to commit to her with everything he had. And he was trying. He had never actually tried before with anyone. He enjoyed making the effort with Klara. He hoped he was doing it right even if he still held her at arm's length. Or further. Much further.

Coward, he told himself.

"Do you mind if we leave a bit early today? I've got something to show you back at the hotel," Chris said, breaking his train of thought.

"Oh, I bet you do," Klara said, giving him a wink that she had been practicing. She tried to be as seductive as Chris, but when she practiced her wink in the bathroom mirror, well, let's just say, it wasn't pretty. She looked more like Popeye coming down with a bad case of pinkeye than a sexy flirt. She thought instead that maybe she should just flutter her lashes. But then again, that wasn't working for her either. She was going to have to remind herself to watch YouTube videos on flirting. There was clearly work to be done.

Chris was on a whole other level with flirting. His filthy mind and his filthy mouth could charm the pants off of anyone. She was slowly learning new tricks, but she was still clueless in the bedroom when she was with him. He was just so damn good.

So damn good, she thought. Her mouth watering.

"That, too." He winked back. Much sexier and much suaver than ole Popeye. "But I picked something up for you. It's for tonight."

Klara's mind raced. She had no clue what it could be. *Should I get him something, too? Does this mean he likes me? Is he making my facial expressions convulse again? Shit!*

"Okay … what is it?"

"Don't you worry about that! Just dress up. Tonight is all about you."

"Me? Whatever did I do?"

"Turned me into a complete and utter fool for you—that's what."

Klara blushed deeply. She felt a bit guilty about pulling away these last few days, but it had given her a fresh perspective on their relationship. Her rose-colored glasses weren't easily cast aside, but she had at least lowered them. If she was going to be disappointed in another man, which seemed to be the case in her life, she was at least going to be levelheaded and prepared this time. She could feel a bit of her heart harden each time she told herself she was going to get hurt. She wished she didn't have to do that, but *que sera sera.*

"What time was it again?"

"Reservations at six thirty. I have a driver, so you can just meet me about five forty-five, and we'll go from the hotel."

"Wait a minute. You need me to get ready in"—Klara panicked, checking her watch—"two hours?"

"What? Is it really three already? Holy moly, time flies when I'm with you! I'd better go get ready myself. I've got a hot date tonight!"

"Exactly how hot is this date?" She stopped to lean down and whisper in his ear as she gathered her things to rush out the door.

"She's fucking fire," he responded as he kissed her good-bye.

He really had no idea how time had gotten away from them. He had too many preparations for tonight. Most of them were already in place, but he needed to pull it off and pull it off perfectly. He had written enough about romance to know what he was doing, but then again, he had no clue what he was doing. His gaze followed her as she hastily exited the coffee shop. Her long hair trailing behind, curling up in the sticky humidity. He wanted to grab that hair in his fist while he took her from behind. His hand gently tugging as she gasped out his name.

Fuck. He had to think of something disgusting to get his woody to go down, so he could rush out the door, too. *Lunch lady at his former high school dancing naked to Bon Jovi?* Yep. He didn't question where his ideas came from anymore. He just embraced it. *Part of being a writer*, he told himself.

Chris let himself go limp and made his way back to his room.

Thank God for housekeeping. That was one thing he didn't have to worry about. The rest of the evening was up to him. He called concierge and put in a few requests for the night. If he was going to pull this off, he was going to have to set alarms like Klara.

Damn her brilliant mind!

The woman might be a little OCD, but she was clever. Chris put an alarm on his phone for a quarter past nine. The time he needed to head back to the hotel.

Sexy-time alarm. He smiled. Anxious to slip those panties off Klara and bury his face between her thighs.

He imagined doing just that as he soaped himself up in the shower. Her sweet pink pussy between his lips. He was going to have to rub one out to keep himself from blowing his top too soon tonight. It had been too long. He knew she hadn't been in the mood lately, but today, Ms. May had gotten released to go home, and Klara had been in a much happier, much hornier place. All morning, in class, she'd traced her fingertips along her collarbone. She'd bitten her bottom lip as she watched him talk. She'd spread her legs a little when she saw him peeking at her while he sat at his desk.

Just in time, too. He planned on giving her the ride of a lifetime tonight. Chris fantasized about how the night would go as he stroked his cock. Imagining Klara on her knees in the shower, looking up at him, smiling with her mouth full of him.

Fuck me … Chris thought as he came quickly. His eyes still closed, imagining Klara swallowing every last bit of him. *So divine. She's so damn divine,* he thought as he cleaned up and jumped out of the shower to get himself ready.

He had just finished putting on his suit jacket when his alarm rang out at five forty exactly, giving him time to do a final glance over before she arrived. *Suit and tie? Check. Nose hairs trimmed? Check. Balls shaved? Check. Cologne? Check. Concierge working their magic while I'm away? Fingers crossed they will.*

Chris had stopped by their desk to give them the bag of candles and goodies for later.

The head of concierge, a woman, had kept shaking her head and praising Chris when they went over the plan. "You are going to make whoever it is in your room tonight be yours forever if you're doing all this!"

Chris had laughed, blushing. He hoped it wasn't too much. He didn't want Klara to run off, thinking he was a loony in love. But was he?

Limerence, Chris. It's limerence. You're leaving in two days. It's limerence.

For a best-selling romance author, he sure did have an internal voice of reason.

The knock at the door came in the exact fashion he'd expected it would.

Knock, knock-knock-knock, knock. Pause for a bit. *Knock, knock.*

Klara never missed an opportunity to be a goofball. It was his most favorite quality about her. A woman who couldn't take herself too seriously? And looked good while doing it? That was a fantasy in itself. Laughter was his own medicine he liked to dish out. It was nice to get it back in return. She got him. He got her.

What's not to like?

Chris answered the door and took a step back, breathless. He knew she was beautiful, but he'd truly had no idea she would dazzle him like this. Klara stood in front of him, her black dress cinched at the waist, subtle but so damn provocative. Her long hair, curled and spilling down her bare shoulders.

Breathe, Chris. Breathe, he thought as his brain quit working.

"You look amazing," they both said in unison. Both laughing, both still unable to move.

Klara had a weakness for men in suits. And Chris in a suit? Add that to the top of the list of her fantasies. His was pretty much molded to his body like a second skin. His trim waist, his muscular shoulders, his tight ass. She wanted to grab that tie and pull him in closer. The longer she checked him out, the more ravenous she became for him.

"Is that ... oh my gosh! It is, isn't it?" Klara's mouth dropped open as she noticed Chris's shoes.

"Blue suede shoes? Why, yes, of course it is." Chris smiled. His eyes sparkling, still taking in the magnificent woman standing in front of him. "Did you know they still sell them? Downstairs, there's a shop where Elvis used to buy his clothes from. I had no idea! It was these or the glitter jacket. I thought you might prefer something a little more low-key."

"They are perfect! Oh my gosh, Chris! Only you and the king himself could pull off those shoes and look dead sexy."

"And one other person," Chris said, handing her two boxes, expertly wrapped in luxurious gold wrapping. "And wait." Chris stopped her before she started opening his gift. "I want you to know, you look absolutely gorgeous. And I knew you would. I just saw this and thought of you, and if you don't want to change, you don't have to. I totally understand. It was just something that reminded me of you."

"Change, huh?" Klara smiled, unwrapping the biggest box first. She was stunned that a man could pick out something as beautiful as the dress that lay in the box before her. White, a creamy white, with a lace bustier trimmed and embroidered in a rose-gold floral-damask pattern. Like a snowflake in the sunshine.

"Do you like it?" Chris said, anxious and excited as a puppy. "Open the other one!" His voice was as excited as a kid on Christmas morning.

Klara was speechless, too overwhelmed to even laugh at his silliness. She opened the other box. Matching blue suede heels.

"How did you ..."

"I checked your shoes like the creeper I am. Your shirt and pants size, too. You were sleeping, and I just had this brilliant idea—"

"You checked my sizes?"

Uh-oh. Chris didn't know if he was treading in hot water or not. He knew there were rules. He wasn't supposed to talk about women's ages, weight, or his preference for the hair on their vajayjay. *Isn't that what they call it? Shit.* He guessed the weight thing probably played into the clothes-size thing. He thought he was suave, but he obviously had a lot to learn.

Klara noticed his smile had started to turn and realized she was about to ruin his night with her sarcastic mouth.

"I think that's the most damn romantic thing ever, Chris," she said, rising up to meet his lips and put on the dress.

Phew. Close one, he thought.

Her spunk would be the death of him, but she was the life of him. Chris helped her unzip her dress and let it fall to the floor. He noticed she wore a matching red lace thong and bra set. He bit his lip and growled as she reached behind herself and grabbed his cock. He turned her around and kissed her hard. Their breathing both getting faster. His alarm blared rudely, interrupting their heat of the moment.

"What is that? Do *you* have an alarm?" Klara stared at Chris, eyebrow cocked.

"Only for tonight." He laughed. "I have a fun night planned. That alarm means we have to get going! Let me help you with your dress and shoes. The driver should be here any minute."

Klara nodded, not wanting to mess his plans up. He'd obviously worked very hard at putting tonight together. She was thrilled, surprised, and feeling a little out of place. He was being really nice to her. Really thoughtful. Really romantic. She wasn't used to this over-the-top treatment. She wasn't saying she didn't want it ... but she was going to have to figure out how to accept it. She was already making a mental list of things she could do to dazzle Chris, too.

Blow job, blow job, anal sex? Blow job. Threesome? Hell no. Too late for that, feelings involved and all! Nope!

Chris had to remind himself to breathe when he looked at Klara in her dress. She sparkled with or without it, but with it, she looked like she could be someone's bride. His bride. Though he would never tell her that. She would think he was nuts. Hell, he thought he was nuts when those thoughts crossed his mind. Knowing her a little over a week and already thinking of the rest of her life with this otherworldly magnificent goddess of a creature? Yeah, he was nuts. All this while he slipped her blue suede shoes on like a damn *Cinderella* scene. He shook his head and hoped that, tonight, he could be half as suave as Prince Charming.

"Let's go," he said, grabbing her hand and kissing it.

The limo parked out front left Klara even more speechless, which never happened unless she had seen sexy six-pack abs. But, now that she was having a taste of the luxurious lifestyle, she realized she liked that, too. The tuxedoed driver opened the door as Chris helped Klara inside. He loved the view from the back or the front or anywhere of her. She was the view.

"Really? Champagne, too?" Klara squealed. "Ahem." She calmed herself and lowered her voice. "I mean, this is cool. This is cool." She nodded.

Chris laughed, knowing it was a bit over the top but taking pleasure in her enjoying every minute of it.

"Let's toast to you, Klara. To being a spectacular woman; to being an amazing caregiver and a kind and loving friend; for being a community-driven individual helping those around you; for being a headstrong boss babe; a go-getter; a tough-as-nails, *don't fuck with me, or I'll cut you yet bake you a casserole* Southern belle. To being my muse, my laughter, my tour guide, and my lover. These have been the best two weeks I've ever had. Thank you, Klara. It's all you. Cheers to you, Klara, the real queen of Memphis."

Well, fuck, Klara thought as she tried her best to hide her tears. *Did he really just say all those things about little ole me?*

No matter how many positive-affirmation Post-it Notes cluttered her home, she couldn't ever make herself feel like Chris was making her feel right now.

"And cheers to you, Chris. You've kicked my ass into gear with my writing, shown me things I've never known I could do in the bedroom … and out." She winked perfectly this time. "And these last two weeks have been the best I've ever experienced as well. So, thank you, Chris, for being just as amazing."

Chris steadied his breathing. *Am I becoming an emotional sap?* He caught himself biting his knuckles as Klara pulled his fist away, opening up his palm, kissing it, and holding it between hers.

"So, tell me where you're taking me," she said, her voice full of excitement.

"It's a distillery turned restaurant."

"Oh my gosh, yes! I've always wanted to go there. The rooster place?"

"Well, technically, I think it's called—"

"The place with the rooster on top?"

"Yes, yes, that's the one." He couldn't help but smile at Klara's excitement. Her pleasure was his.

Her eyes danced like a kid in a candy store. The neon signs reflected in them each time they passed another bar, another restaurant. Flickering stars was what it reminded him of. She had stars in her eyes.

"You know they have the best vodka ever? It's the artesian wells in Memphis. Our magic water."

"Is that what it is? Something in the water here? That's where all this magic comes from?"

"It must be. Liquid gold. Let's test this theory out tonight with some of their drinks. I hear their craft cocktails are amazeballs!"

"Amazeballs, eh? Count me in. Anything that makes you say amazeballs, I'm game."

"I'll remember that. You just cursed yourself there. Lots of chick flicks, mud wrestling, spa days, shopping sprees. All amazeballs."

"I agree, all amazeballs … with you," he said, finishing his glass of champagne just as they pulled up to the restaurant.

The hostess, obviously a fangirl, greeted Chris with the warmest of welcomes. Her hand shook his a few seconds too long, her eyes lingering to his left hand, checking for a ring. Klara knew. She had done it, too. She let the ladies look, drool, giggle. He was hers tonight, and he let everyone know the same.

He stepped aside to let Klara follow the hostess to their table, gently guiding her with his hand on her lower back. He couldn't help but touch her. She was the most beautiful woman he had laid eyes on, and she was all his. Their table was tucked in the most private spot, as per his request. Dark, candlelit, intimate. Flowers on the table, the server attentive and waiting already to greet them.

"This is so damn amazeballs, Chris. Wow. I feel like I'm in a Hallmark movie."

"I've been feeling that way since we met at the park. Hey, whatever happened to Farmer John? Do you still see him running?"

"Farmer who?" Klara teased.

"That's what I thought," Chris growled, running his hand up her thigh and along her panties under the table.

Klara liked it when Chris was growly and rough but only because she knew he was the biggest sweetie pie outside of the bedroom. If he pulled any controlling bullshit on her in their relationship, they both knew, he probably wouldn't want to set foot anywhere near Memphis again. She had met her fair share of those so-called alpha males. No, thanks. Chris was a dream, and he didn't need to be a cocky asshole to prove it.

"Ooh, jealous, are we? You do know, Farmer John doesn't have shit on you. Not my Chris." Klara knew as soon as she said it that it was probably a dumb remark. *My Chris. As if.*

"Your Chris?"

Klara looked down into her cocktail, stirring it and shrugging her shoulders. "If you want—"

"I like it when you talk like that. I'm yours for the taking."

"Is that so?"

"It is."

"All mine?"

"All yours."

Klara was ready for the check and to head back into the bedroom. This man was making her melt, and he had barely touched her. But he didn't even need to. Just being near him set the hairs on the back of her neck standing straight up. She could feel the electricity between them both. And, by the way he was watching her, he could feel it, too.

"Tell me what your plans are when you leave," she said, taking a long drink from her cocktail and feeling brave. *Is this liquid gold or liquid courage?*

"I plan on going wherever my calendar tells me I have to be and stopping here for you every which way possible. Would you like to come with me sometime? Whenever your schedule permits? I would love to experience new sights with you."

"I'll see, but I'm pretty tied up with work and this last semester. It would be nice to get out more though. I just don't see it being possible much for me right now."

"I understand. We'll figure it out." He winked.

The conversation drifted back to their novels, writing, favorite authors, favorite movies. They got to know each other little by little, silly story after silly story, sad times after sad times, stress after stress, achievements after achievements. Klara learned Chris had wanted to grow up to be an ice cream truck driver. Chris learned Klara had held a job as the mouse mascot for a local kids entertainment place. The suit she described as smelling of peed-on nachos and sweaty ball sack. Chris said he'd had a teacher that smelled like that once and mused that maybe he worked evening hours for the same children's place.

They discussed philosophies, music, favorite travel destinations, and dream vacations. Phobias: Chris apparently freaked out over balloons, and Klara was the normal one for once and just hated spiders. Goals: they both wanted families and to settle down as writers. Pet peeves: Klara had had enough of people not using their turn signals, and Chris didn't like hearing people chew.

As they lost track of the time, Chris and Klara discussed anything and everything, exploring each other's lives. The conversations were amazing, the company was amazing, the food was amazing, the drinks were amazing. Everything was perfect for the both of them, especially Klara. She was on cloud eighty-two this time.

"I've got more surprises up my sleeve," Chris said as his phone alarm buzzed. "Up for some more fun?"

Chris motioned for the check. The waiter had already cleared their table a long, long time ago. They had finished their food and had been sipping cocktails and talking for the last two hours. The lively crowd around them was drowned out by their complete focus on each other.

"The answer is always. With you, always."

"Come with me," he said, pulling her chair out and offering her his hand.

Chivalry isn't dead, I guess, Klara thought as she grabbed his hand and followed him back to the limo. She wondered what more he could have possibly thought about as the driver took them through the city streets and toward the water front. The limo slowed to a stop by the riverbanks. Right in front of the iconic Hernando De Soto Bridge, lit up in a brilliant light show.

"You see that twenty-fourth top cable from the right? Count them."

"Okay. Yeah, I think so."

"Okay, now, count down four lights."

"Okay."

"That's yours."

"What do you mean, it's mine?"

"I dedicated it to you. It's the Klara Woods light. Check it out."

Chris pulled out his phone and showed Klara a picture of the dedication.

"*To Klara. You are my light. My true Memphis queen,*" Klara read aloud, weakly handing his phone back to him. "I don't know what to say, Chris. Thank you. That doesn't even seem to be enough. You are ... this is ... it's a dream."

"You don't have to say anything. I just want you to know how I feel about you," Chris said, pulling her toward him and kissing her lips. He pulled back, searching her eyes, hoping she knew the words he wasn't brave enough to say.

"I know," she whispered back. Gazing straight back into his eyes.

They stayed until the show ended and then headed back to the hotel room. Both of them starting to feel frisky. Teasing and caressing each other in the back of the limo.

They barely made it to the room when Chris remembered what was waiting.

The concierge! He crossed his fingers that, when he opened that door, things would be exactly as he'd asked the staff to help him make it.

And it was. He was blown away just as much as she was.

Candles and roses filled the room. They lay on top of the desk, the tables, the armoire, the nightstands. Champagne was chilling next to the bed, and soft music drifted from the radio. This was definitely a Hallmark movie.

"Wow! How did you do all this?"

"I had lots of help."

"I bet you did," she said, awestruck. "This has been the most romantic night of my life, Chris. Really, you outdid yourself."

"Come here. The night isn't over yet," he said, wrapping her up into his arms and slowly unzipping her dress. He took every piece of clothing off of her and admired the masterpiece before him. "You are a work of art, Klara," he whispered into her ear, setting her on the bed.

She watched in a daze as he slowly undressed himself. Their eyes locked on one another. He could hear the catch in her breath when he finished undressing and stood naked. His cock pulsing. He needed her, and she needed him.

His hands caressed every inch of her body as he kissed her from her forehead down to her ankles. His tongue explored as he sucked and licked and moaned between her thighs. The taste of her, the scent of her, the feel of her. He could feel his whole body go warm as he made his way back up to her mouth and kissed her deeply.

Klara closed her eyes. Her breaths in sync with his. His breaths in sync with hers. They tangled themselves together. He was in oh-so deep, and she held on oh-so tight. Their hands intertwined as they squeezed, their knuckles turning white. They found their rhythm in slow, deep thrusts.

Klara knew, if bodies could become one, theirs had. She had never had sex like this before. She had never made love. She felt Chris deep. Under the layers of her anxiety. Under the layers of her guilt. Under the layers of her weaknesses, her quirks, her losses. That was where he nestled. His body, his soul, his pulse, fluttering into her and filling her with a euphoria she'd never experienced before.

Chris felt it, too. She was an extension of him. Where his cock stopped, he really just kept on going, melting into her. His brain buzzed, the hair on the back of his neck rose, his cock throbbed, his spirit sang. Klara slowly gyrated her hips to match the gentle bobbing motion that Chris danced inside her. Their pulses matching, their motions matching, their heartbeats matching.

With their whole selves in perfect tune together, the world disappeared around them, drowned out by Klara's blissful sighs. She could feel her legs begin to tremble. Her whole body quivered as she wrapped herself around Chris tighter. Her fingertips leaving marks on his back as she gripped him hard.

"Come with me," she whispered, breathless and high. The fantasy-like night had awakened all of her senses at once, and she needed to let herself go. She could feel the buildup in her body, her mind, her breaths, and her heart.

Chris nodded, unable to talk and unsure of what was happening to him. His whole body trembled, too. His mind was in a state of ecstasy, where all he could hear were her whispers, all he could see were her fluttering eyes, all he could taste were her delicious lips, all he could feel was his Klara.

They held each other tighter as he gave the last few thrusts he could manage before they cried out with a feeling that was new to them both. The heat rising from where they were joined and spreading throughout their entire bodies.

The world slowly came back into view as they lay, silent, and overcome with emotion. Neither speaking, afraid to break the spell.

TEN

The last two days had been a blur. Klara and Chris had been spending every waking moment together since date night. Something changed in them both. They'd either lost themselves or found themselves that night. Klara, of course, had found herself. She knew, without a doubt, that Chris was the man for her. And she also knew, without a doubt, that she was the woman for him.

But does he know I'm the woman for him? How can he not?

That night had shaken them to the core. The depths of their souls. The air had turned to glitter, they'd breathed it in, and both of them couldn't stop sparkling. At least, that was how she felt about it.

See what this is doing to me?

She was hot, she was cold, she was hot, she was cold. She was hot, hot, and hotter, and she melted. She gave up being rational. Wasn't she supposed to let herself go this week? Didn't he want to reward her for being such a good girl on her promise to live in the moment and quit being such a spaz? If he did, he made no mention of it. By the looks of him, Klara could tell, he was struggling with his own thoughts, too. He'd talked about limerence roughly five hundred seventy times in between date night and today—the day he was leaving.

"Remember the plan. Okay?" he said, holding her hands and staring into her eyes.

"I know; I know. Communication is key."

"Definitely. I'll only be gone three weeks, and then I'll have three days here. Off again for a few more weeks and back. Maybe you can fit in a beach trip when I fly back home somewhere in there. Even if I'm not there and you need to get away, go for it. You're always welcome in my home."

Klara sat quietly as he started to pack his bags. Slowly folding his clothes. Taking his time. She contemplated sitting on his luggage and crossing her arms like a brat, but he would just pick her up and throw her on the bed and ... *hmm*. She contemplated it again.

"You okay?" He noticed her eyes were glazed over, staring into the distance.

"Yeah, sure."

"What are ya thinking about?"

"The other night."

"Ah! That was ... something."

Something, she thought. *Just something.*

"It was," she whispered. "Actually, Chris, it was more than something to me. I've never felt that before."

Chris sat back down on the bed, sighing loudly. "Me either. I don't know what it was or what it meant, but I know exactly how you feel."

"Do you?"

"Of course I do. I feel the same way. You know I'm completely infatuated with you. The limerence effect."

"Oh damn, enough with the limerence!" Klara rolled her eyes.

Chris's body stiffened. He should have listened to Marcy. She was right. He'd thought he was being logical. Romantic and logical. *A smart woman like Klara would appreciate logic, right?* It was not like she wanted to give up her career and run away either. He hadn't exactly been leading her on. He'd told her that he wanted to keep this up and see where it goes.

"What's that supposed to mean?" he said, testing the waters.

"What do you think it means?"

"I don't know; that's why I'm asking. You don't feel the same way?"

"No, I don't," Klara sighed.

Chris could feel his heart plummet into his stomach. *What the fuck is going on?* He stopped what he was doing and waited for her to explain.

"Chris, I don't limerence you. I love you. Is that not obvious? Do you feel this between us? Do you know what that is? That's not limerence. Sure, we are infatuated, and that shit doesn't last ... but this? The support for each other, the trials with this long-distance craziness, all that. That is love—or at least, that needs love to make it work. It's a choice. Love is a choice. And that's how I feel. Not this bullshit limerence. I feel love. I am choosing love. I am choosing you."

Klara had had enough beating around the bush while he was beating around her bush. She was tired of the unknown, the tiptoeing, avoiding the uncomfortable conversations. The emotions of the last week coupled with their transcendental lovemaking session and, now, having to let him go—it was all too much for her. She knew she should have kept her mouth shut, but she just couldn't. She had known this could cause a fight or that she would come off as some clingy, crazy cat lady. Even though she didn't have cats. All the hair in her condo was from … well, who the fuck knew? But that was beside the point. She wasn't crazy. She was in love. And damn it if she was sick of not shouting it to him from the rooftops.

Chris lay back on the bed, rubbing his hands along his face, closing his eyes into a deep squint. Hoping that he would just blend in with the bed and disappear. "Klara … I don't think that's how you feel."

"Are you trying to tell me my own feelings? Are you saying I don't know how I'm supposed to feel?"

Shit, Chris thought. He was. He didn't know what to say or what to do. He just knew he was in an insane amount of discomfort right now.

"I'm sorry. I'm just trying to say, I don't know if I'm there. I care about you so damn much. I just don't want to hurt you or get hurt myself, I guess. I've not been in love. If that is what I am feeling, so be it. But I can't tell you that unless I know it's true, and I don't even know how to tell if it's true. How do I know a feeling I've not experienced?"

"You just know. And, if you don't just know, then you just don't. Look, I wasn't expecting you to say it back. I understand you have a fear of the L-word. Your parents didn't exactly model what a loving relationship was to you, so—"

"Whoa, whoa, whoa. Wait a minute now. You're bringing up my childhood? Are we fighting?"

"No!" Klara's face was flushed, her hands on her hips, her lips pursed. She looked ready to attack.

He should have never brought up the limerence thing. Things had been going too well. He hadn't expected to set her off. He didn't want to. It was hard enough, leaving, but now, it would be even worse.

"I'm really sorry, Klara. I have strong feelings for you. Can you trust me? I'm trying here. I might not be in the same place as you. I don't know why. Yeah, it's probably some of my parents' fault but also mine. I haven't ever been available. Day in and day out, I've been working. You know how it is. This type of relationship. It's new to me. I've never had this type of feelings for anyone. I just don't know what to say."

"You can start by not saying limerence. Women want to know they are more than an object for your fascination."

"That's not what you are to me at all!" Chris said defensively.

Does she really feel this way? After all I've done to try to show her how I feel? Even if I can't say that four-letter word?

Klara knew she was getting out of hand. Maybe she was doing it on purpose. It would be a lot easier to let him go if she was pissed off at him. That was how it usually worked with her. They'd made her mad, and she had let them go. Except Chris wasn't making her mad really. It wasn't his fault. Not all of it anyway. So, he couldn't commit. *Wait, he didn't say he couldn't commit. He said he didn't know how he felt.* She was getting flustered and confused.

"Are you able to commit to a relationship with me?" she asked, determined to find out where she stood.

"Yes! That's what I've been saying. I want to give this a try. Me and you! Have you been listening? We were just talking about the plan. Communication is key and all?" Chris was flustered, pacing back and forth, unsure if he wanted to run away now or grab Klara and show her with his body how he truly felt.

Why are words so hard for me? I'm a writer, for goodness' sake! It's not the words; it's the emotions, he reminded himself.

"Okay."

"Just okay."

"Okay, I'm sorry I spazzed out," she whispered, barely audible. Her hands were covering her eyes, so he couldn't see her shame.

Chris laughed. "Come here, you," he said as he pulled her onto his lap. *Crisis averted?* "I might not be able to give you what you want yet, but if you just give me some time, I'll do my best. I'll try to be more open with you, too, so you know what's going on in this head of mine. I can make this work, Klara. Promise."

"Promise?"

"Pinkie swear." Chris stuck his pinkie out and grabbed hers. Intertwining it with his own and giving it a kiss. "Come on, my little spaz kitten. I've got to get to the airport. Walk me out?"

Not trusting her voice to waver, she just nodded and followed his lead. She didn't want to open her mouth anymore. She clasped her lips shut tightly, hoping that she wouldn't cry. He couldn't see her like that. He'd already seen her spaz out. She was surprised he wasn't running away and not looking back. At least she knew now for sure how he felt.

Klara could see through the glass doors that Chris's driver was already outside and waiting on him. Her palms started to sweat, and she wasn't sure her knees could make it to the door. Thankfully, Chris held on to her tight, slowly leading the way. The driver tipped his hat at Klara, greeting her with a smile. She nodded, still unable to talk.

"Klara"—Chris gently cupped her face with his hands, bringing her gaze to his—"thank you for telling me how you feel. Thank you for being transparent and honest with me. You're not a spaz. You're just not dead inside like me." He laughed, trying to lighten the mood.

The familiar sadness enveloped them both. She could see it in his eyes, too.

"Thank you for the lessons, Chris. And for the memories," she muttered into his mouth as he kissed her, gentle but rough. Wanting, needing.

"There is a lot more where that came from. Until next time?" His eyes searched hers, his fake smile beaming. He didn't want to leave on a sad note. Even though he ached as if he was leaving his heart back in his hotel. With her. His Memphis queen.

"Until next time." Her voice trailed off.

She averted his eyes and stepped back, letting him turn to go. He ducked his head into the car and shut the door. Rolling the window down to give her a wave as the driver sped off.

It was done. Over. She could go home now.

Home, she thought. *He is home.*

When Chris was gone, life was very different for Klara. Her return to reality, she knew, would never be the same. Although he had made good on his promises. So far. They communicated daily through texts, video chats, phone sex, and he even sent her limerence letters though the mail. Within a week, her mood was lifted but only a tiny bit. She still missed him terribly. Her days and nights were no longer spent in his arms but back in her condo and in front of her laptop. She had typed the last sentence of her first novel yesterday and proudly sent Chris a text.

It's done.

What's done?

My novel. First draft is finished!

> *Holy shit! That's amazeballs, Klara! Got an editor in mind? Because, if you don't, I know a guy. Just sayin'.*

Thanks, Chris. I'll keep that in mind!

Klara could use his resources, but she knew then this big accomplishment she had wanted her whole life wouldn't exactly be hers. She needed to do this for herself. Without help. Partly because her pride and stubbornness, partly because she was a badass boss babe.

Over the next few weeks, she kept herself busy with writing, writing, and more writing. She started running again and taking on extra shifts at work. Anything and everything to keep her mind off Chris. She ached for him. Literally. It was as if a hole had been left in her chest. She thought about filling it with wine and credit card debt, but she knew that wouldn't leave her satisfied very long either. Only Chris left her satisfied these days. Very, very, satisfied. So satisfied that she contemplated buying him a clone-a-willy kit, so she could always have him around.

Klara decided she needed to do something drastic to get her mind off her love life. Something life-changing. Something to keep her even busier. *A baby? Hell no. Not yet anyway. Not unless it's Chris's babies. You know ... we had that one slipup on date night and didn't even bother with condoms.* She wouldn't be shocked if she had fallen pregnant from that night. That was some beautiful baby-making sex they'd had! Stupid of her to get lost in the moment and not use protection. But, no, thankfully, her period had been in full swing after that. Exactly after that actually. Four days early. She liked to think it was her uterus crying out for missed opportunities. *Vengeful little shit.*

Klara mused, *What to do? What to do? A tattoo? No. A skydiving trip? No. Cut my hair? No. Dye it? No. Adopt a cat? One step forward into crazy-cat-lady land? Maybe.* She would be well on her way into old-lady territory in no time. Klara wondered if she needed to also buy pearls and pantyhose. She was feeling more than her age these days with her late-night writing and early morning running anyway. She spent too much time in the morning gazing in the mirror and pulling her face this way and that. Maybe, if she could have a lift here, a tuck there. *Is that a wrinkle? Already?* Fed up, she would slather on her sunscreen and head out for a run to clear her mind.

Klara had missed too many running sessions while Chris was in town. Her stamina had quickly tanked after he left. Especially since she had eaten her feelings the week after he left. Cupcakes, ice cream, fried pickles, French fries dipped in milkshakes, wine, and maybe a tequila shot here and there. Typical breakup food. Except they weren't breaking up, so she really had no excuse. She couldn't fill that hole with food either. Damn, she wished Chris were there to fill her hole.

She thought about reaching out to old friends she'd lost touch with, but that was just too creepy, too. They would probably think she was trying to sell them on a pyramid scheme if she suddenly popped back up in her life after years of silence.

Here, try this blow job–proof lipstick or these sticker-nail-polish kits, which aren't trashy at all, right? Ever heard of this drink? It makes you ten pounds lighter by blowing out your asshole. No, really, that last part isn't true. Wink, wink. Beauty is pain. Embrace it.

No, Klara couldn't reach out to any old friends. They had their lives, their families, their careers. She didn't want to be a third wheel. The loneliness she'd had before Chris she could handle, but now that he was gone, she had to reach out to someone. A therapist would be a good choice, but Klara didn't always make the best choices. Instead, she joined a running group. Exercise could be therapy. It certainly would give her that endorphin high that she missed getting from Chris.

Klara bent down to double-knot her laces when she saw him making his way toward her. She saw his abs first, of course, and then his smile. Farmer John. Of course he was part of this running group! How could she have doubted that? Her luck and his body?

"Hey! Not flying solo anymore, I take it? Is this your first time?" He smiled down at Klara, sticking out his hand to greet her. "I'm John, by the way. I know we've met before, and I still feel terrible about that morning. I didn't hurt you, did I?"

Klara almost fell over. *His name really is John. Farmer. Fucking. John. Oh boy.*

"Not at all. That was partly my fault, too. I wasn't paying attention. It's fine. You're fine." *You're fine? Shit ...* Klara's mind was doing it again. *Zapped.* She couldn't contain herself when she caught a glimpse of a hot body. Even though she wasn't calculating how fast he could get her panties off anymore or dreaming about how he looked on bended knee with a fat rock in his hand, ready to make her his. No, she wanted Chris like that. But Farmer John was nice eye candy, so she let herself relax.

"It's my first time in a group, yes. How about you? I usually see you flying solo, too."

"I joined a few weeks ago. Best decision I ever made. Well, not the best, but a damn good one." He shrugged.

"Well, now, I'm curious. What's the best?"

"My farm. Making the decision to do what I love instead of what society thinks I'm supposed to do."

"I thought I'd seen you at the farmers market before. You're the one with the homemade pastas, right?"

"I am." John smiled. "All organic, all fresh. Have you tried any yet?"

"Not yet. I'm not the best chef. I'm afraid my pasta skills are as fancy as ramen, and that's it."

"You literally just drop my pasta in boiling water, too. I'll show you. I'll be at my stand Saturday morning if you want to drop by."

His eyes searched Klara's. She didn't know how to respond. Was he hitting on her or just being friendly? Was she cheating on Chris if she said yes? She wasn't into Farmer John anymore. All she wanted was Chris. What could be the harm?

"Deal. I could use some healthier foods around my place."

"Perfect! Good luck on your run. It's a great group. All experts, so no crashing into each other." He winked.

He winked. He winked. He freaking winked.

Klara steadied herself. *What the heck have I gotten myself into this time?*

The farmers market was within walking distance of Klara's house. She usually stopped by after an early morning run, picking up a few essentials. Sometimes, she would pick up a few extra goodies to drop by Ms. May's house. Anything to make Ms. May's life easier since her hospital incident. Even though she was an old windbag, Klara couldn't bear to lose the old lady. She had been more of an ear than even her own mom these last few years.

The smell of flowers lingered in the air as she made her way past the florist's stalls, making a mental note to keep pressuring her boss to open their own stall. She was looking for a way to get the older residents, like Ms. May, out and about. She thought, if they could sit and work a stall, they would be happy. Not only would they be in fresh air and moving their old bodies around for exercise, but they would also be earning a little extra spending money.

Klara smiled to herself, proud of her ideas. She had been full of them lately. She'd sent her novel off to the editor a few days ago, and so far, she had received really positive feedback. She had even been put in touch with an agent and told to get started on her next story, which she had and was quickly powering through. She needed a pat on the back. *A gold star. A bottle of expensive champagne. A night on the town. A celebration. A ... kitten?*

"Hey there," John called out to her from behind his stall. His hands were full with not one, but two squirming kittens.

"Hey! Wow, you have your hands full! Who are these little cuties?" Klara asked, reaching out to hold one.

A hot man holding kittens? Just shoot me now.

She was dead. D-E-A-D.

"These are my new furry friends. Someone dropped them off at my farm, I guess. Found them all in a cage. We're keeping one, but we couldn't keep all of them. These are the last two that need homes. Sweet little things though. Need a cat?"

Klara noticed he'd said *we*, and that was when she noticed another farmer hottie behind John, unloading a truck. She could tell through his tight shirt that he was just as blessed as John. His eyes the same blue, his five o'clock shadow looking like it would feel amazing, scraping against her freshly shaved thighs. Who was he? A brother? A coworker? A friend?

"Actually ... " Klara's attention went back to the squirming rascal in her hands. "You know what? I do. I really do."

"Really? Are you sure? That was pretty easy."

"I've been toying around with the idea of becoming a crazy cat lady, so yes. I think it's a sign you have some available. I guess it means I'm ready to become a fur mom after all."

"Ha! You are far too chic to be a crazy cat lady! Fur mom, yes. Crazy cat lady? Doubtful."

The man unloading the truck made his way to the table and started to unpack boxes and boxes of pasta and sauces. Klara got a faint whiff of basil, and her stomach started to growl.

Oh no, don't do this again, she thought, sending the message down to her stomach.

"Oh, hmm ... I didn't know kittens growled. That's odd," John said as he inspected the kitten.

Klara laughed it off as if she had no idea what he was talking about.

"They don't growl! They purr. Don't ya, you wittle wascal?" the farmer friend said to the kitten in John's arms.

"This one is a rascal for sure," John said as he put the squirming kitten back in the cage. "Klara, this is my partner, Grayson. Grayson, this is Klara. She's a part of the running group, and she has graciously decided to take one of these fur babies off our hands."

Partner? Like a farming partner?

"Nice to meet you, Klara. And thank you! I like you already. I'm a cat lover for sure, but I swallowed a cat hair in my smoothie today, and no, ma'am, not again! One is enough. John wanted to keep them all, but someone has to be the voice of reason," he said, winking at John.

Oh ...

"I've got to get these boxes down to the recycle bin. Have fun with the new addition, Klara," Grayson continued, kissing John on the forehead and scurrying off.

Klara noticed John's gaze follow his partner until he was out of sight.

"Right, so back to these things. Which one do you want?"

"I'll take both," Klara said, stunning herself.

The realization that Farmer John was gay had her brain frazzled. Not that she was interested anymore, but all those proposal fantasies, poof! Gone! She couldn't wait to get back and text Chris all about it.

"Really?" John asked, wide-eyed. A part of him was sad to see the kittens go, but a part of him was relieved.

"Sure, why not?"

"Twice the poop. Twice the food. Twice the hair balls."

"I can handle it. Plus, it's lonely at my house. I think these two will liven it up." Klara smiled. If this didn't work out, she would just chalk it up to another bad decision. She was used to those by now.

"Lonely, eh? No way! Not you. There's no special someone to help you with these two wildcats?"

Klara blushed. How was she going to explain this one?

"Well, there is. You've actually met him before. It's just ... "

"Wait a minute ... I've met him? Is he part of the running group?"

"No." Klara shook her head.

"Is he a regular here? A customer of mine?" John said, probing for details.

"No ... " Klara shook her head again.

"Well? What's his name?"

121

"His name's Chris. He was the one who, um … helped me when we crashed into each other. That was actually how we met."

"Holy shit! Seriously? That guy? He was very … very … good-looking. And chivalrous, obviously. Saving you from me and all." John laughed. "So, you two are a thing now, huh? Wow. That's a hell of a way to meet someone. Like a sappy, romantic comedy movie. I love it! Where is he now?"

"That's the thing. He doesn't live here. He's a long-distance … friend."

"Friend? Long-distance? What?"

"He's a writer and an instructor. So, he travels a lot. And, yes, a good friend. I don't know what else to call him at this point, I guess."

"No? Well, us men are hard to figure out. Maybe, next time you see him, he can give you more clarity."

"Maybe … "

"I've got an idea. How about you come to the farm? Wait, when is the next time you see him?"

"Next Friday, he's coming into town."

"Okay, hmm … how about next Wednesday? You available, say, around six? You can come to the farm and have dinner with me and Grayson. We can teach you how to make an awesome dinner for your long-distance lover that will knock his socks off and have him tied around your pinkie. Consider it a huge thank-you for taking these rascals off my hands. Plus, I have a lot of cat stuff you can have. Grayson will be so happy to get rid of it all!"

Klara had no idea how she had come to the farmers market to pick up a few bits of fruit, and she was now leaving with two cats and a date with two very attractive gay men. Her Saturday was turning out to be really good or really bad. She wished Chris were here to see all this.

"I can do Wednesday. I'll move some things around. Should be fine. Are you sure? I might be a fire hazard in the kitchen." Klara shrugged. She was nervous already.

"Definitely sure. Favor for a friend. I owe you for almost knocking you down that day anyway. Though I'm glad it turned out the way it did! Now, you and Chris have become a thing. Klara and Chris … Klaris? Chrisara?" John mused, confused. "I'm going to need to work on this couple's name. You two aren't making it easy."

"Oh, yeah? Hmm ... " Klara played dumb, although she already had been working on it since the beach trip. She'd tried every combo, and none had the cute, witty ring to it that would be front and center on their wedding blog.

"Nah, not like my and Grayson's. Everyone knows us as The Johnson. Which doesn't bother me one bit." John smirked.

Klara laughed loudly. She was really beginning to like Farmer John even more. Maybe, one day, she would tell him about her nickname for him. *Maybe ...*

The kitten in her arms was fast asleep against her chest, purring. The other was pacing back and forth in the cage, calling out for someone to entertain her. Klara knew that cat was going to be trouble.

"All right, I'd better get going. Looks like I'm going to the pet store today and settling two fur balls in their new home. Not quite what I was expecting to pick up at the market, but I'll take it. They are just so damn cute, aren't they?"

"Yep. And I'm so glad they are going to a good home. I know you'll be a great fur mama. If you need anything, anything, here's my number. Text me yours anyway, and I'll send you my address for Wednesday. Here, I've got a travel cage in my truck. Let's put them inside. Easier to carry."

"Okay. Thanks. Wednesday it is. Date with The Johnson," Klara said, raising her eyebrows.

"Ha! Hope we aren't too hard for you to handle!" John laughed.

Klara's mouth watered. But just a tiny bit.

ELEVEN

Klara wasn't even in her condo for an hour before she realized it wasn't kitten-proof. So far, the kittens had knocked over two vases and one picture frame, clawed her office chair, and thrown up on a rug. What in the hell had she been thinking? She hadn't even had time to sit down and text Chris about her day. These two heathens were constantly getting into something.

"Listen up!" she barked as the kittens ignored her. "You two are going to have to behave. My house, my rules. Shape up or ship out!"

One of the kittens pawed at the flowers Klara had growing on the windowsill. Klara quickly picked her up and put her down by her feet, giving her one of the toys the worker at the pet store had recommended. She sat down, exhausted, and checked her watch. Doing the mental math to calculate what time it was in California, where Chris had been all week.

He should be awake and moving by now. She knew he had an early flight to catch. She checked her texts again. No *good morning* text? Not much of anything lately actually. His communication had been spotty at best the past week, and although Klara knew he was busy, she couldn't help but wonder. She'd never been to Cali, but when she thought about it, all she could think about were beautiful, tall, and tan blondes, fashionistas, supermodels, women who lived on kale and ice chips and could send anyone ... *Chris* ... to his knees.

She imagined him going out for drinks, his fangirls getting giggly, him whispering in their ears the filthy things he'd whispered in hers. Them being his new "muses," as he'd said. How they would so easily spread their legs for him.

I mean, who wouldn't? He is walking sex on a stick. With a big stick. No gherkins. Klara was stuck in between annoyed with the lack of communication and feeling randy, thinking about Chris's pickle, when her phone rang. *Finally.*

"Hey, gorgeous! Good morning! How is it going? How's your day?"

"It's been ... fine." Klara decided to hold off on telling him all of the excitement. At least until she knew why he had been flaky this week. "How was yours?"

"Just fine? Nothing exciting happened? Mine was all sorts of exciting. Rushing to get to the airport, waiting at the airport, eating shitty airport food, waiting even more at the airport. And here I am."

"Well, that sounds terrible! I'm sorry you've had to deal with all that. I would be a frantic mess."

"You would. But I'd calm you."

"You already do."

"The feels. The feels," Chris moaned, clutching his heart.

"All the limerence feels ... " Klara shot back, feeling feisty.

"Ooh. I walked right into that one. Practically handed it to ya. I'm going to be there in exactly six days, and I plan on putting all these feels to good use. I want to feels in your mouth. Feels in that tight little pussy of yours. Feels those lips between my teeth. Feels myself slide right into you."

Fuck, he's good. Klara could *feels* herself starting to get wetter.

"I want to *feels* you, too. I didn't get much *feels* from you this week. I know you're busy and all but—"

"But communication is key, and I've been slacking. Totally. I get it. And I want you to know I'm sorry. I did spend every moment I could reaching out though. I just didn't have many moments. Marcy has been rearranging my schedule, and my agent has been toying with different opportunities for me and not leaving me alone about it. I've just got a lot going on. I'm so, so sorry. I promise this week will be better. I think. Gonna do my best. And hey! I'll see you soon, and we will make up for any missed time. Deal?"

"Deal," Klara muttered.

She was still annoyed. His excuse didn't make her feel any different. Sure, he was busy with important stuff, but she also wanted to be important stuff. Not knowing where she stood was getting old. Really old.

"Hey, I've got to run. They're boarding. I'll call you when I land. At least, this week, I'll be in your time zone. I think it will make things easier."

"Okay. Bye, Chris. Safe travels."

"Bye, sexy."

Klara hung up the phone, her brain recounting the conversation. *Does he miss me? Is he growing distant from me with all the distance, or did it make him want me more? How does he feel now? And why can't he tell me?* She wouldn't make the mistake of telling him her feelings again. Putting herself out there had made her feel way too vulnerable.

The feels ...

She sighed. She was going to package them up, stuff them in a box at the top of her closet, and forget about them. She had two babies that were going to keep her mind off of things and two new friends. She decided to keep her new friends to herself. If Chris showed more interest in her life, maybe she would then tell him about them, but after the funny feeling she'd had last week, she was building her walls up again.

Chris could hear it in her voice. Klara was upset with him. He knew he had been distant this week, but he wasn't sure why. He was busy; that was true. But he was also ... *scared? Nervous?* He didn't know. All he knew was that he missed her, and this long-distance dating was so damn hard. He woke up, thinking of Klara. He went to bed, thinking of Klara. He spent every waking hour thinking of Klara. Klara, Klara, Klara. She was constantly on his mind. He could barely concentrate at work. His mind kept wandering to Klara and what she was doing. Those nights at the hotel, especially their date night. He had been like a teenager again with all the erections he kept getting every hour on the hour when he thought of her.

He knew this couldn't be healthy. How happy he had been there, with her. Just being in the same city as her even. *But now?* Now, he was here, and she was there. Now, they were apart, and he was lonely. He hadn't been very lonely before he met Klara. Sure, he'd had his moments here and there when he wished for a lover to share his time with. But, for the most part, Chris was happy with his career being that partner. Now, his career was cold and gloomy. His writing was suffering without her. How he wished he were back at that coffee shop, writing beside her now. Breathing in the scent of her, like honeysuckle and wildflower. His legs rubbing up against hers under the table. His eyes on her lips as they broke into a smile.

He needed Klara, and he was scared. What if he wasn't able to do this long-distance thing? He was already spazzing out. She'd told him she loved him before he left, too, which definitely didn't help matters. He couldn't hurt her, not Klara. Not anyone. He wasn't that type. He hadn't asked to be in a relationship; she'd just kind of fallen in his lap. Or right in front of him anyway.

Chris closed his eyes and rested his head back, hoping to catch some sleep on his flight. Trying to read or write would only prove useless. Both of those things suffered now that she wasn't around. Klara had shaken his life up, both good and bad. He wasn't used to this. He needed his career. He needed Klara, too.

How can I have my cake and eat it, too?

"Excuse me?" a woman's voice called from next to Chris as she gently tapped his shoulder while he stared at the ceiling, unable to sleep.

Chris turned to the woman, startled.

"Is this you?" She pointed to his picture on the back of one of his novels.

"I'm afraid it is." Chris laughed. "When I was about ten years younger anyway."

"Ten? Ha! You don't look a day over twenty-five. Not with that hair and that smile," the woman crooned next to him.

Chris couldn't help but notice how beautiful she was. Her skin sun-kissed, her hair golden, her eyes as blue as any ocean he'd ever seen. Chris suddenly grew uncomfortable.

"Well, thanks, but I, uh … it was a long time ago. But, yes, I wrote the book. Is this your first book of mine you've read?"

"Nope, definitely not. I'm a fan. I've never paid attention to the back covers though until this one. I always had in my mind that you would be ... oh, I don't know ... someone a little ... less attractive?" the woman said, biting her lip.

"Really? What made you think that?"

"Well, all the fantasies you write about. I always thought it was a man who wasn't able to play out those fantasies, so he wrote about them. But, now, I see I was mistaken. I'm quite sure you could have anyone you wanted," the woman purred again. "I'm Leslie. Nice to meet you, Christopher," she said as she stuck her hand out to shake his.

"Nice to meet you, too, Leslie," Chris said.

He could feel himself growing hot. *This woman is coming on strong.* He checked his watch. Three more hours in the air.

Crap! This is going to be a long flight, he thought.

He couldn't believe a drop-dead gorgeous woman was hitting on him, and he wasn't even interested. In fact, he was extremely uncomfortable. He'd never been in this situation before. Attached and unavailable even though he knew he was still available ... kind of. It was not like he was married or anything. He caught the woman trying to get a glimpse of his left hand. *Ring check.* He had seen it before several times. Hell, he had done it several times.

"So, Christopher, working on anything exciting now?"

"I've got a few ideas I'm kicking around. I've mostly been teaching lately. Writing has kind of taken a backseat while I get some things done. But I always have a story going. I think that's true for any writer. Whether it's in our heads or on paper," Chris rambled. He was trying to keep the conversation friendly and even a little boring.

"I'm very much looking forward to reading what you come up with next. These last books of yours were ... extra steamy. You sure do know how to speak to women. I'm assuming it's mostly women reading your books," Leslie said, fanning herself with his book.

"Thank you! My readers *are* mostly women. But I only know how to write about talking to women because I get a lot of help from my ... girlfriend. She is always good at letting me know what women want," Chris replied, hoping she'd get the hint.

"What a lucky woman to have someone like you whispering in her ear. So. Lucky." Leslie grinned.

Chris smiled back at her, watching her lick her lips.

Nope. Girlfriend didn't stop her, Chris mused. He racked his brain to try to come up with something to steer the conversation away from his erotica. *Damn me and my sexy skills! Why can't I do something not sexy? Like sell vacuums or be a butcher. Those aren't sexy at all. Sucking force and beating meat. Hell!* His brain was wired for erotica.

"Oh no! I'm the lucky one. She's my muse."

"Muse, eh? So, you do write from experience." Leslie smirked.

Chris blushed and could feel his body go warm again. He wished this lady would give up. It wasn't happening. If it wasn't for Klara, he would hop on her, and his next novel would have some Mile-High Club scenes, but … Klara. This lady was beautiful but not as beautiful as Klara. This lady was interesting but not nearly as interesting as Klara. This lady smelled great but not divine like his Klara. No, she wasn't Klara, and he wasn't interested.

"All experiences with her. Yep."

"What a life she's living. What … a … life." Leslie shook her head in amazement as she pulled out her headphones and popped them in.

He guessed she'd finally gotten the picture. Though he did catch her constantly readjusting herself as she read his book. He could practically feel the heat coming off of her.

Chris laid his head back again and closed his eyes, smiling as he pictured the way Klara had looked that day in the garden shed.

Yep. What a life …

T-minus two days until he gets here, Klara thought.

She had set a countdown alarm on her phone, which she checked every forty-five minutes. She couldn't believe it was almost time to see him again. Her thoughts often drifted to that first moment they would greet each other. Her mind was so deep into him that, when she finally came home at night, she wouldn't be aware of what she'd even done that day.

What happened at work? No clue.

What did Ms. May do today? No idea.

What did I eat? Couldn't tell ya.

What did Chris say? She knew that word for word. She often went back to read all of his texts several times a day, tending to overthink things.

I wonder if he meant this when he said that, or I wonder if he really wants this instead of that. Does this mean what I think it means? Is he just telling me what I want to hear? Her mind raced.

Thankfully, with her first book finished, she decided to take this week off from writing. She would have been absolutely useless anyway. The kittens were driving her up a wall, Chris was communicating more now but still too damn spotty for her taste, and she had to prepare her place for his stay—not to mention, prepare herself. Wax, shave, run, hair—all of that. She was exhausted already. She was really looking forward to tonight, the night that she got to be with The Johnson.

Klara giggled anytime she thought about their couple name. She often said it out loud and made herself laugh. She still hadn't told Chris about them. She instead told him she was meeting with friends from her running group, which wasn't exactly a lie. She planned on telling him everything when he came back into town. Same with the cats. He had no idea she was a mom now. She hoped he wasn't allergic. He would fall in love with them, just like she told herself she would, too, one day—when they stopped clawing her furniture. She made a mental note to ask The Johnson about that tonight. She was new to cat ownership and had no idea what to do. They were cute when they were sleeping at least. Until they woke up and swatted her nose like a fly so that she got up to serve them breakfast.

"You two, be good. I don't trust you yet. You both have been little shitheads lately. I love you. I'm out!" Klara said as she quickly shut the door behind her, locking them in her bedroom.

She had put the cat litter box in there, food in there, and all their toys. Checked it two, three, four times for cat-proofing basics she'd read up on and turned to forget about them before she could take a step out her front door. Except she felt terrible.

Damn. This must be what mom guilt feels like, she thought, pausing to turn around and let them run free like the wild animals they were. She heard a faint meow through the door. *Be still my heart!*

"Mama will be back soon, little peanuts!" She marched forth, wine bottle and bouquet in hand like a proper dinner party guest.

The drive to The Johnson wasn't too bad. It was farther than she normally drove, but Klara didn't mind. Long car drives to her meant solo concerts. She cranked up the music and belted out every love song she came across. She rolled the windows down and sang to the cows she passed, the flowers, the sun slowly setting in the sky. She imagined Chris next to her, singing those same love songs to her.

Except he couldn't because, ya know ... love songs ... and, well ... he doesn't love me. Limerence.

Klara could feel herself starting to get annoyed again, thinking about his limerence bullshit and how he'd acted when she told him those three words. She didn't regret it. Okay, she did. Just a little. But she didn't regret saying them. She only regretted being the first to say them. *And what if we broke up? He would know I was a heartbroken little girl who had fallen in love, and he would just be okay? Would he be okay? Who knows? Emotionally unavailable men! What did I get myself into?*

"You are a lady after my own heart, missy!" Grayson greeted her, taking the bottle of wine and the flowers. "A true Southern belle! And is this a French wine? *Je' t'aime!* John likes it more Italian, of course. I mean, look at me! Of course he likes Italian. But ... *personnellment, je ne suis pas d'accord. Vive la France!*"

Klara stood, mouth slightly dropped open and unsure of what Grayson was saying, except she did know he'd just said he loved her. *And damn it, if this hot Italian gay man I just met could say he loved me, why couldn't Chris?*

"Let's crack this baby open then, shall we?" Klara grinned.

"Charmed. I'm so damn charmed. And smitten. If I swung that way, Klara, you'd be the first to know!" he said, linking elbows with her and leading her up the front porch and inside.

Their home was exactly how she'd imagined it. An older antebellum home on a few rolling acres. The dream. This was the home she'd thought she would have with John. Their kids playing in the front yard as she sat on the porch, sipping her sweet tea. The smell of jasmine in the air as they swung in the porch swing, laughing about the time they'd met down by the river. She almost laughed out loud at the absurdity of her fantasies with John. She hoped she didn't get too drunk tonight and spill it.

"Oh, Johnny! Look what the cat dragged in!" Grayson called out, leading her down a hall and into the kitchen.

"You're a cat now, huh? I would have thought you were more of a tiger," John replied, smirking at Grayson.

"Rawr," Grayson growled, smacking John's ass.

John stood over a pot of boiling water. His hair disheveled, his eyes narrowed in deep concentration.

"Come here, Klara. Check this out," he said, turning toward her.

She noticed he was wearing an apron. One of those silly ones with the six-pack abs outlined on it.

"Love the apron! I'll not be able to focus on cooking with those abs in my face." She smiled.

"Don't I know that!" John laughed.

Klara made her way around the rustic table, noticing the brick, the copper, all the fragrant herbs drying in the windowsill. It was exactly as a home should be. She wondered if they had a spare room upstairs, so she could move in. Just her and The Johnson. And the cats.

Ugh, the cats. She glanced over her outfit again, checking for cat hair for the eighth time.

"My pasta doesn't take long to cook because it's fresh. The secret to cooking it is knowing when precisely to drop it in the pot, which is just when it reaches a rolling boil. Not too subtle, not too feisty. Like yourself," he said, nudging her with his elbow.

"Not too subtle, not too feisty. Got it. What kind of pasta is this? It smells divine!"

"Mushroom sage. Made fresh this morning!" John beamed. He clearly had a passion for this. "Grayson made the brown butter gravy this morning, too. We'll just warm it up and serve it over the noodles. Super easy. He's my sauce man."

"So saucy!" Grayson snapped his fingers in the air. He already had the flowers Klara had brought in a vase, the table perfectly set, and was pouring the wine. "I also baked the bread, made the salad, and helped Chef Johnny Boy here harvest the herbs."

"Don't know what I would do without you, Mr. Gray!" John smiled, slowly stirring the pot of noodles.

"Mmmph! You know I like it when you call me that!"

"Oh boy, do I!"

Klara giggled at the friendly banter between The Johnson, her eyes glazing over as she wished Chris were here to laugh along with them. She missed him so much, and the time apart was making it harder and harder and harder. She was excited to see him, but she knew a lingering sadness would weigh on her all weekend, knowing that he was just going to disappear again.

"You okay, honey?" Grayson asked.

Grayson and John both were staring at her.

"Oh, yeah, sorry. I'm fine."

"Nope. That look was not fine! That look was the look of something or ... someone on your mind. Come sit, drink, tell us about it." Grayson pointed at the chair beside him.

"Go ahead." John nodded. "I'm just warming the gravy in a skillet. The noodles are about done. I'll teach you more in a bit. You clearly need a drink."

Klara smiled shyly. Right now would be a good time to have a poker face. She let out a sigh and sat down beside Grayson, taking a long sip of her wine. She explained to them her situation. The meet, the class at school, the hotel, the beach, the date night, the limerence. Her voice stopped shaking after her second glass of wine and her second helping of pasta.

"So, you're telling me ... Chrissypoo ... is all of a sudden being more distant now? And he was the one who said communication is key, right?" Grayson said, his mouth parted in a pout.

John had seen him take in the drama. Grayson lived for this stuff.

"Yeah, he did. But I think I might be pulling away some, too."

"Totally understandable, honey! You don't want to get hurt! You're going to have to ask him straight up when he comes this weekend. *How do you feel? Where is this going? Is this enough for you?* Because you're really asking if you're enough; we both know that. Except you might not want to just come out and say that part. Or maybe do it. Hell! Go all in. No sense in living your life in this limbo. You could be meeting all sorts of fantastic men out there. Don't put your life on hold for a hot-and-cold, long-distance relationship that might never be," Grayson said, leaning back and crossing his arms.

"It might never be, but it could also be. He might be the one. Let's not be too hard on him. Most men have a rough time with opening up. I know I did, and I think Grayson will tell you I still do sometimes. I'm working on it, but undoing the way I've dealt with life isn't a quick, overnight thing," John chimed in.

Klara looked from one to the other. Her face flushed from the wine. *I'd better stop now or else I'll really spill the details,* she thought as she took a long drink of water.

"You're both right. I think I will ask him this weekend. I can't live like this, and I don't want to put life on hold for a what-if. But, if he's willing to work on being more transparent, then, well, we'll see."

"You don't have to put your life on hold. Just have him in the background for now. You do you. Get that book out, finish this last semester, be the rock star you are—with or without him! I'm so damn anxious now to see how this goes!" Grayson said.

"Me, too!" John grinned. "Same thing this time next week?"

"Deal," Klara said, still trying to sober up for the long drive home.

"We have a guest room, ya know," Grayson said, noticing her water glass was empty. "You don't have to chug it like a linebacker."

"But the cats … " Klara started.

"Let me tell you something about cats; they are so self-sufficient. Did you feed them? Do they have their litter box? That's all they need, mama. And you need some time for you. Come on. Relax and hang out. Guest room is prepped and ready anyway. Might as well use it!" Grayson said.

John nodded in agreement.

Klara hesitated. She was feeling mom guilt again. But she also really wanted to see his guest room. She could only guess it was fabulous. She wondered who had done the designing, Grayson or John. Her money would be on Grayson, but John had fabulous taste, too. They really were perfect. The Johnson.

"Okay. If you insist."

"You bet I do! Slumber party!" Grayson jumped up. "Come on. Let me show you around!"

The rest of the evening was spent with great wine, great food, great company, great conversations, and tons of laughter. Klara was sure she would wake up with sore abs from laughing so much. It had been a while since she laughed like that. Tears were streaming down her face. Grayson was animated and lively, and John even joined in on the silliness.

The perfection of the night sent her into a happiness coma. Klara didn't even remember what time she went to bed. She just remembered crawling into crisp cotton sheets and falling straight to sleep. Warm, safe, happy. She didn't even think of Chris or check her phone the entire night. She was too busy frolicking with The Johnson. Left completely spent and satisfied.

TWELVE

Klara? You okay?

Klara, I'm worried about you. Haven't heard from you all day! What's going on?

I hope you're safe. I'm thinking of you. Please call me when you get this. No matter what time. I just need to know you're okay.

The messages on Klara's phone jolted her awake and into a panic. Four missed calls, too.

Shit!

She must have hit the Do Not Disturb button at some point during the night. The wine making her brave and stupid yet again. Except not too stupid. She was safe in bed on an amazing farm, in the middle of nowhere, with the smell of bacon calling to her from the kitchen below. The only thing that would make this more perfect was if Chris were next to her.

Chris ...

Klara wasn't sure what to respond back. She felt terrible for not communicating with him. She gathered up her things and decided to head downstairs and get back home first. She needed to clear her mind and think. Plus, that bacon smelled damn good.

"Good morning, sunshine!" John said, hovering about the stove. "How do you like your eggs? Fertilized?" He laughed, handing her a plate.

"Uh-oh. I can only imagine the shenanigans I talked about last night. Don't tell me. I'll go crawl in a hole now."

"Uh-huh. You are quite the source of entertainment." John laughed, placing a cup of coffee in front of Klara and watching her practically inhale it.

"You're such an awesome friend. Thank you for this. All of it. I didn't realize how much I needed some time away and to think, laugh, socialize, and just be me."

"We all need that from time to time. You're welcome here anytime. The Johnson cures all."

"It really does!" Grayson said, groggily entering the room, wrapped in a leopard print robe with a matching eye mask on his head that read *Nope*.

Klara already wanted to be his new BFF.

"How are you feeling, hon? You okay? Gonna be ready for that big date tomorrow? Got your ducks in a row? Or at least, in the same pond?"

"I think so. The plan is, butter him up with a fabulous dinner, thanks to y'all … give him a couple of glasses of wine, make him quiver until he can't feel his legs in bed, look at him with puppy eyes, and take the conversation to a serious level."

"I have taught you my ways, young Padawan. Go forth and conquer." Grayson beamed. He loved a good project, and being the hopeless romantic he was, he was going all in this with her.

"But take this with you." John handed her a large paper bag full of pasta, sauce, bread, fresh veggies, herbs, catnip, and even candles.

"Everything you need for tomorrow night, except that French wine. Go get another bottle of that. The exact one. It went perfectly with the pasta. Text us if you need anything, too. Any questions about anything. And I do mean, anything," Grayson said with a nudge.

"You guys are way too good to me. Seriously, this is the best. What gracious hosts you are!"

"Well, if you haven't noticed, Mr. Drama Queen here is rooting for you. We both are, but he lives for this shit. We want a happily ever after for both you and Chris. Grayson might have taken his wedding magazines out last night after you went to bed."

Grayson let out a gasp of horror. "Mr. John, how dare you! I have no idea what you're talking about. I'm an innocent Southern belle, and I don't partake in these types of shenanigans!"

Klara laughed, overwhelmed with emotion for her new friends. She wondered if Grayson would be so nice to her, knowing that she used to flip through the same magazines on occasion while planning her own wedding to Farmer John. She had a feeling he would laugh and tell her, *Hands off, bitch!*

"I'll let y'all know if the plan worked as soon as he leaves. Again." She rolled her eyes. "I gotta get back home to my babies!" she continued, picking up her things to go. "Thanks again. So much. For the food, the fellowship, the hospitality, the shenanigans."

"Anytime, Klara Pie!" Grayson said, kissing her cheek good-bye.

"Come on. I'll walk you out," John said, picking up her bag of goodies and carrying it out for her.

It was still early when Klara arrived home. Her long drive had given her time to think about how to respond to Chris.

Honesty is the best policy? Mostly.

She needed to see his reaction to the plan before she let him further into her life. She loved him, and if he couldn't love her back or wouldn't love her back, she had to let go. For her sake.

She settled the frantic kittens, letting them crawl all over her to calm her nerves. She closed her eyes, practiced some deep breathing techniques, and called him. He answered on the first ring.

"Hey you! Are you okay? I've been worried sick about you. I thought something happened with you or Ms. May again ... or I don't know what! What's going on?"

Klara knew that, if Chris was this upset, he surely felt more than just limerence for her. *But why, oh why, can't he admit it? Why do I have to force it out of him?*

"I'm so sorry, Chris! Here, I'll show you. Check your texts." Klara sent over a picture of the kittens. "Meet Ernestine and Hazel. They've been keeping me on my toes and so busy! Plus, I've been getting ready for tomorrow, and I guess I just overwhelmed myself." *It's not a lie if I just omit a few details, right?*

"You got a cat! Or ... cats! Oh my goodness, they are adorable. I love the names." Chris instantly recognized it from the brothel turned restaurant they'd messed around in.

"They are adorable balls of pains in my ass. Should have named them Hemi and Roid."

The silence on the phone was deafening. Klara thought maybe she had gone too far. Again.

"Good God, woman." Chris laughed. "You have such a way with words, and speaking of words ... I finished my novel, too, last night. So, I guess we're both in the stages of publishing."

"That's awesome, Chris! Let's celebrate tomorrow night! I'll make you a special dinner at my place." Klara couldn't believe her luck. The plan was falling into place easier than expected.

"That sounds amazing! I can't wait for that. Are you as good in the kitchen as you are in bed?"

"You'll have to see tomorrow."

"I plan on it. You know, I woke up rock hard, thinking of you grinding on my face while you watched me play with myself. I need you in my mouth. I so need to touch myself for relief, but I'm saving it for you. I want to give it all to you. Everything."

"I'm pretty sure the waistband in my panties just sizzled off, but I guess I'll save mine for you, too. You're so damn fiery. Tomorrow is going to be amazeballs. I can't wait to see you. And, again, I'm so sorry my communication sucked yesterday."

"Mine's been pretty spotty, too. I understand. We're both busy."

"Yes. Busy, busy. Can I pick you up from the airport tomorrow? Or will you have a driver again?"

"Driver. I'll come straight to your place. No worries. I'll be there right at dinnertime to enjoy a home-cooked meal. I'm so looking forward to that! And to having you for dessert!"

Good, Klara thought. Because she didn't even plan for dessert and wasn't even going to attempt to bake a cake. She thought she had a canister of whipped cream in her fridge she could squirt on her thighs, but she couldn't even remember when she'd bought it. It was probably putrid at this point. That would be a terrible idea. She reserved herself to cleaning out her fridge and cleaning up her entire house today as soon as she was back from work.

"I'll be ready and waiting. I've got to run though. I need to put a few hours in today. Text you soon. Promise."

"Tell Ms. May I said hi!"

"I will."

"Oh, and, Klara? I miss you."

"I miss you, too, Chris," Klara stuttered before hanging up.

His sudden confession of his true feelings sent her into shock.

Maybe he is working on his issues. Maybe he is going to tell me he loves me now, and we'll ride off into the sunset. Maybe ... just maybe ...

She let herself fall into the rabbit hole. Her outlook on tomorrow night suddenly became much more positive and much more hopeful.

It was a little after three when Klara finally made her way to Ms. May's house. She had pruned, watered, and weeded every other house on the street, saving the best—or the worst, depending on how you looked at it—for last. But Klara preferred to love the old fart. Even if it was like driving a sharp tack under your fingernail.

"You got a twinkle in ya eye. That's dangerous. He must be in town." Ms. May was sitting on her porch, waiting her turn with Klara. Even in this heat, she already had two sweet teas poured, ready for the latest gossip.

"Not yet. Tomorrow though," Klara said as she plopped down on the rocking chair next to Ms. May.

"Has he told you he loves you back yet?"

"No, but I did get an 'I miss you,' so that's a first step, right?"

Ms. May sighed. "So, what's next? He gonna just come here, get the goods for free, and leave again? Y'all spending the rest of your days like that? That's a nice arrangement for him! You know what we called those types back in my day? Cake eaters! He can have his cake and eat it, too. Klara, quit baking for this man until you get some solid answers on where he wants to go. Go about your own life and let him choose you. If you're too busy when he makes his wants clear, then oh well! No harm, no foul. It's only gonna get harder, baby."

"I have been going about my life. He's just been in the background. All the damn time. But ... enough about him. I landed an agent, and she's pitched my book to four different publishers. She's guaranteeing me one will bite, so ... I could be a published author soon. Now, you can say you know two people who are famous!" Klara could hardly contain her excitement.

Her life goal would be complete at only twenty-six. Now, she just had to learn how to make a career of it. She was sure Chris would help her figure it out. He was the pro after all.

"Do I get a signed copy? You got me in there? You dedicating this thing to me? Ain't I your muse?" Ms. May suddenly looked excited. She could picture herself the talk of the church group, rubbing shoulders with the famous and all. Certainly not the rich and famous. Not yet anyway.

Klara looked as skinny as ever. She needed to feed that girl a pork chop.

"I'll sign you a special dedicated copy ... if it goes through and someone actually believes in it enough to publish it. I believe in it, but I'm no publisher."

"I believe in it, too. And I'm pretty smart, so ... you'll get your time to shine."

Klara almost teared up. She thought this was the first time she'd ever heard Ms. May say something so nice to her before. She hadn't even told her own mom about the book, knowing it would be picked apart and deeply criticized. She was so grateful for the people in her life. Her small circle she had now was ever supportive of her endeavors. Even if Chris did decide it wouldn't work out, she knew she had people who would support her. No matter what.

"Ms. May, I do believe you have a heart in that cold, dead body of yours."

"I don't know what you're talking about, missy. Now, here, cut some of those roses and put them on your table tonight. See if he asks where they came from. You'll know if he's interested then."

Klara laughed. Another scheme? How come her other relationships hadn't been this complicated? Of course he would think they were from work. Maybe.

"All right, you conniving ole fart! I'll give your trick a shot. I'll add it to my plan," Klara said, getting to work on the rose bushes.

"Your plan? What's this? This the first I'm hearing about a plan!"

Klara told Ms. May all about The Johnson, the food, the romantic dinner tomorrow night, followed by the puppy eyes. To her surprise, Ms. May thought it was brilliant. She also wanted to meet The Johnson.

"They seem like my kind of people," she said, laughing as Klara recounted Grayson's one-liners.

"The Johnson is definitely your people, Ms. May. I'll bring them by sometime. Promise. They would eat you up."

"Everyone loves a crotchety ole granmama. Now, come inside and let me bake you some cookies for tomorrow. You tell him you made them."

"That would be a lie! He knows I can't bake!"

"Is he a cake eater?"

"I don't know—"

"Yes! Now, hush your mouth. If it makes you feel better, you can help me. But my cookies ain't ever turned a man away. One bite of this lovin' from the oven, and he will be hooked. Take you outta that friend zone; you just watch. My grandbabies call them my crack cookies. So, come on in and taste this crack." Ms. May laughed and slapped her knees, proud of herself for that one.

Klara just shook her head in pretend shock. She could see she wasn't going to win this argument, so she let Ms. May lead her inside and teach her Baking Crack Cookies 101. With a side of sass. How could Chris resist?

Chris was packing for his trip to Memphis when he got the call from his agent. Her voice blubbering on and excited.

"A huge opportunity, promote your new book, movie rights," his agent rambled on. But all Chris heard was, "Europe, Asia, one year, maybe more, see the world."

He was thirty minutes from hopping on a plane to see the woman he finally thought he would be able to settle down with, and now ... and now ...

He told his agent he would think about things and give him a call next week. But he knew. He already knew.

143

Klara had just turned soft jazz music on in the background and lit the taper candles that John had given her when there was a knock at the door. For some reason, she was anxious. More anxious than excited. She was hopeful that the night would go according to her plan, but she still had this nagging feeling. The feeling of reality and loss. That, even if things did go well, he would be gone again in a heartbeat. With her heartbeat.

How did I let myself get so tangled up in this man? Her heart sank into her chest when she heard the doorbell ring again. She was stalling.

"Coming!" she called out, racing to the front door, dodging kittens, and doing a quick once-over to make sure her house was acceptable.

All day, she had spent cleaning, and all afternoon, she'd spent setting things up. She'd never gone above and beyond like this. Not even for herself. It was kind of nice. She thought she would do it more often. Maybe invite The Johnson over or even Ms. May.

"As stunning as ever," Chris said as soon as she opened the door. His lips were on hers in an instant.

"Well, hello to you, too, stranger."

"Damn, I've missed you. This is for you, compliments of Marcy," he said, handing her a bottle of champagne. "I've got something for you, too, but you'll have to wait until later for it."

"Oh, I bet you do." Klara smiled. She was already eager to get him back into bed. His skin on hers, his breath on her neck, his lips ... everywhere. "I'll chill it for tonight. That Marcy is so sweet!" she said, motioning for Chris to step inside.

"She's super proud of you for finishing your novel. She said she will need an autograph next time you come down."

Next time, she thought. Things were already going well.

"Oh, hello!" Chris smiled as he leaned down to greet the kittens.

They instantly circled his legs and rubbed themselves against him.

"Wow, they really like you. They don't even greet me like that much. They more ... swat at me."

"Ha-ha-ha-ha! It's the primal tigress in you. They're just treating you like one of their own. Playful little things."

"Uh-huh. Not sure I believe that line of thought, but okay. Come on. Dinner is on the table."

"For me? Really?"

"All for you. I've missed you," she whispered in his ear, taking his hand and leading him into the kitchen.

"Me, too," he replied. "Wow, you have a really nice place. It's so fresh and spring-like in here! Those flowers! Beautiful! Did you pick those yourself or …"

Bingo. He cares, Klara thought, stifling a giggle. She would have to tell Ms. May her plan had worked.

"Actually, Ms. May gave those to me, which reminds me … have a seat and try one of these," she said, handing him the plate of cookies.

"Dessert before dinner? I'm in!" he said, taking a bite of the cookie and moaning out loud. "Wow! These are better than the best ever flavor in the world—chocolate chip!"

"I'm more of an oatmeal-raisin gal, but I'll let that slide … and thank you. I thought you'd like them."

"Seriously? Well, I knew you had to have one fault at least. Guess we've found it. I thought that was an old-person favorite. Raisins? In cookies? What are you trying to make a dessert healthy for? By the way, can I have another? These are dangerous. Addicting even."

She laughed. "Sure, sure. Enjoy. I'll pour the wine and get to serving. I made this pasta that will knock your socks off. Fresh Memphis pasta."

"You already knock my socks off but Memphis pasta? I'm intrigued. I thought Memphis was only known for barbecue."

"So much to learn, Chris. So much to learn." She kissed him on the forehead and got up to make them both plates.

They toasted their wine to each other, broke the bread, and spent the next two hours laughing and catching up. Klara caught him up on Ms. May, her work, her novel, her running group. Not on The Johnson. She thought it was too soon to bring up attractive men even if they were gay. She got the feeling it wasn't the right time. She didn't want to talk about anyone really other than themselves. But, sticking to the plan, she was slowly putting Chris into a food coma before becoming all sexual deviant and doe-eyed.

"A beautiful woman like you, making me such an amazing dinner? I love my life," Chris gushed. "I'm really impressed by the music, the candles, the wine, and especially the food. It's so very *hygge*."

"*Hygge*? That's the trendy word right now, meaning cozy basically, right?"

"Yep, it is. Brushing up on my foreign languages. You should try it. It's a great, big world out there! You need to see it all. I think you'd love it!" he said nervously, his foot shaking under the table.

How am I going to break this to her? Should I do it now? Later?

"Maybe one day. But, for now, what I really want to see is, all of you," she said, leaning across the table and playfully biting her finger.

Later, yep. I'll definitely bring it up later.

Chris stood up from his chair and slowly undressed as Klara's gaze took him in. He took everything off. Everything. Until he stood there, stark naked, erect, and hungry for dessert.

"You can have all of me," he whispered.

Her eyes widened. *Chris is such a damn rock star. I would have never been brave enough to pull that move off, but Chris? This man is on another level.* Her knees were already getting weak, and she hadn't even touched him yet.

"Let's go," she said, hurriedly blowing the candles out and yanking his hand toward the bedroom.

The room was already dimly lit with five of those knockoff, fake candles flickering away. Klara was prepared, as usual. And, despite the wine, she was still nervous.

"Bring the champagne," he muttered to her, his mouth on hers.

Klara ran back into the kitchen to get the champagne. Chris was already in bed, looking comfortable, upon her return. His hand stroking his cock as he licked his lips. Her jaw dropped.

She put the bottle on the nightstand and slowly began undressing herself with her best strip-tease moves. She had on black lace lingerie under her dress, the bra cups exposed, letting her breasts spill over.

"You're so damn gorgeous. And I'm so damn lucky," Chris said as he reached up and pulled her down on top of him.

She could feel his hard cock in between her legs as she straddled him, rocking back and forth. Her lingerie grew wetter and wetter as she rolled her hips across his full length. He lifted her up and flipped her over, crawling on top.

"I want to taste champagne off your neck, your nipples, your navel, and this sweet pussy of yours," Chris whispered to her, dipping his fingers inside her and bringing it to his mouth. "Can I do that?"

Klara, struck dumb again, could only nod.

"Mmm, you're my whole damn fantasy, Klara," he said, popping the top on the bottle and drizzling it over her. "Your bedsheets might be a little sticky," he warned.

"Let's make them a lot sticky," Klara begged.

Chris growled as he made his way down her body, kissing her, licking her, tasting her.

Klara's hips rolled into his lips, her wetness grinding on his mouth as he sucked the champagne off of her.

"Mmm, Chris. You like that? You want it? Tell me you want to taste me explode into your mouth."

Fuck, Chris thought. *Klara is definitely on her A game tonight.*

"I want to swallow every last drop of you, Klara," he said, putting his hands under her hips and burying his face deeper into her. "Give me that cum, baby. Show me how much you like it."

Klara's legs began to shake as her hands gripped the bedsheets with her fists. Her body was losing control as she bucked against his tongue inside her, his hands firm and steadying her as she became louder and louder and louder. She lost control as wave after wave after wave slid down her body and out into his mouth.

He looked up at her, smiling. His lips wet with her.

"I'm not done yet. Come fuck me," she said, tossing a condom over to him.

"Damn, you're a wild woman. *My* beautiful, wild woman. Mine," he said as he slipped the condom on and thrust inside her, hard.

His hands grabbed her ankles and pushed them back into the bed as he dipped deeper and deeper inside her. He could feel her still pulsing around his cock. Her lips parted and gasped with each hard thrust. He couldn't last long, not looking into these mesmerizing eyes, not with her sweetness on his lips, not with the way she moaned while grabbing his ass and pushing him down into her harder.

He kissed her just as he came. His mouth stifling her moans as he grunted and buried himself inside her. Both of their bodies twitching. Their heartbeats racing up against each other.

He rolled over beside her as they both tried to catch their breath, looking at each other and laughing.

"That was fucking hot!" she said, her face alight and flushed a bright pink.

"You're incredible! And I mean that in every single way. The perfect woman!"

This is it, Klara thought. This was the chance she needed. While the dopamine was flowing. She needed to know. To make plans. With him. She had to go all in.

"Chris?"

"Yes?" He turned toward her. A look of concern overcoming his face. He could tell it in her voice. Something had changed drastically. *Is it the champagne in the bed? Is she ... oh God ... is she pregnant from that slipup on date night? Oh no. Should they be having crazy sex like that with their baby inside her? But she has been drinking ... no, she wouldn't do that. Not Klara.*

"I have something to ask you." She sat up on her elbows, hovering over his chest.

"Okay." He hesitated. "I actually have something to ask you, too."

"You do?" Klara tried to contain the excitement.

Maybe, tonight, I've proven I am wifey material. Maybe he's finally come to his senses. Maybe. Just maybe.

"Actually, let me grab it real quick. It's in the bag I brought in."

"Okay." She nodded.

Is it a ring? Oh my gosh, I'm going to be a fiancée. She couldn't wait to call The Johnson and gush over how all this went down. Leaving out the details, of course, except for the champagne. *That was hot!*

Chris was back within a minute, handing her a heavy bag.

This doesn't feel like a ring, she thought as she opened the bag and pulled out two travel guides, a passport cover, and a printed plane ticket receipt.

"What's this?" she stuttered. Confused. Her dopamine high quickly wearing off.

"It's your ticket to see the world! With me! I've got an overseas book tour. We're going everywhere! Starting in Europe, ending in Asia. Let's call it a sabbatical for you. Of course, you'll be able to write along the way. Probably even better than you could here, being inspired by other cultures and all."

"This ticket is for next month. I start school right after this. Remember ... my degree?" she said, slightly annoyed.

Chris picked up on the tone in her voice. He knew she had school, but he thought maybe she could put it on hold. It was a once-in-a-lifetime opportunity. They would be great travel buddies. He'd thought she would be ecstatic.

"Look, I know it's sudden. It's sudden for me, too. I only just learned about it yesterday. But I had to jump on it. It's a great career move! For the both of us!"

"For the both of us ... yeah ... " Klara set the ticket down and got up to get dressed.

"Yes, for the both of us, silly. Don't you want to get out and see the world? You said so yourself at dinner!"

"I said, one day ... not next month. Not when I've just kicked off my writing career and I'm finishing up my degree! How long will you be gone?"

"Uh, I don't know ... "

"How long?"

"A year ... minimum. Depending, I guess, on what cities sign on last minute and whatnot. Nothing is set in stone, except my departure date. That's kind of nonnegotiable. Agent's orders. You know how those agents can be. Bossy, bossy."

She sat on the bed, trying to gather her thoughts, trying to hold her heart together, trying to steady her voice and not shout or cry or get angry. *I can't believe I thought he was going to marry me. He knows damn well I can't go. This is just an easy and cowardly way out for him. The famous Mr. Christopher Kaiser. Touring the world, one muse at a time.*

"I can't go, Chris. Sorry. And I don't see how this is going to work long-distance anymore. I'll not do it to myself. I love you. You know that. I told you. You can't even make a commitment to me, yet you want me to give up all I have and come backpacking across the continents with you?"

"We wouldn't exactly be backpacking. My agent's been booking some really nice hotels," he tried. "Of course I don't want you to give up everything for me. You can come home anytime you want actually! When you are tired of it and get homesick. Just say you'll think about it, please? I don't want to lose you. I know you think, whenever I talk about limerence, it means just that, nothing. But it means something to me. I'm doing my best."

Klara thought that Chris's best just wasn't good enough anymore. She wanted to tell him to roll his limerence up and shove it up his ass, but instead, she played nice. The night was already ruined. She didn't want the last weekend with him forever to be ruined either. That was what she got for letting down her walls and letting Mr. Superstar in anyhow.

"I'll think about it. But I don't see it working."

"Okay. Thank you for thinking about it at least," he said as he leaned down and kissed her forehead. He was hopeful, but like with his decision to leave, he already knew. This was the last time he was going to see Klara. He all of a sudden was dizzy. He'd made his choice, but he hadn't prepared for this. "Was there something you were wanting to ask me, Klara?"

"I already forgot. It was nothing, I guess. I'm pretty tired though. Gonna do a quick rinse in the shower and change the sheets, okay? You can watch some TV or do some work while I get the bed ready again. Make yourself at home."

"Can I join you for that quick rinse? I'm all sticky, too," Chris said solemnly. He could tell she wanted to get away from him.

He was no good at this relationship thing. She deserved better. He suddenly felt two inches tall and ashamed to even be next to her.

"It's a tiny shower. I'll come get you when I get out. Deal?" Klara didn't want him seeing her cry. She needed some time alone to go over what had just happened and what the future held for her now.

A few minutes ago, she had heard wedding bells, but now, all she heard were funeral bells. *His funeral.* Because, if she stayed here much longer, looking at him, she was going to send him into an early grave.

Chris nodded, knowing she needed to be alone and away from him. He knew. He already knew.

THIRTEEN

Chris had really messed up this time. The whole weekend had been awkward with little mention of what was to come next. He tried to bring up the trip again, but Klara only said she was still thinking about it. Of course he knew she had a career she was working on, but he still held out hope that she would throw caution to the wind and come along on this adventure. Selfish, he knew. He couldn't exactly pass up this opportunity though. This was a once-in-a-lifetime offer.

She has to understand that, doesn't she? I can't just pass this up, can I?

The way she was somber, quiet, and definitely not herself told him otherwise. He did all he could to put them back in the moods they had been in before he told her about the offer. He took her back to The Peabody for a rooftop drink, they went shopping together for Ernestine and Hazel, they went for a run together, they made love all hours of the day and night, and he even cooked her his special breakfast—chocolate strawberry crepes. But, no matter what Chris did or said, Klara was still in another world. Her gaze looked right through him. Her lips turned up into a smile that didn't reach her eyes. *A fake smile.*

He glanced over at her as she sat beside him on the couch. Her hand lazily digging in the popcorn bowl. Bowl to mouth, bowl to mouth. It was almost as if she were a robot. Her focus on the TV in front of her and nothing else.

What is she thinking?

"Klara?"

He seemed to have broken her trance, as she slowly turned her head toward him.

"Yeah?"

"I leave tomorrow."

"I know."

"We haven't talked about the travel," he said, taking her hands in his and commanding her attention.

"I know that, too," she sighed.

"I kind of need to know something. I really hope you say yes. I don't know how—"

"How we will date with you on the other side of the world? It's impossible, and honestly, I'm not putting myself through that. I can't wait around on you. How is that fair to either of us?"

"I know; you're right."

"And, another thing, what about my school? You think I'll just sacrifice all of my work to run around and support yours?"

"No, not at all."

"Look, I'm sorry if I'm coming off a little bratty. But I thought this was real. I thought *we* were real. I mean, I told you I loved you, Chris! And, now, you'll be so far gone; it's almost as if you'll have never existed."

"Don't say that! Of course what we have is real. You know how I feel about you."

"Oh, do I? Because you don't ever say anything, except you have limerence for me. Limerence, and that's it. That isn't love, so I can see where your opportunity was such an easy choice for you to make."

"But it wasn't an easy choice. At all."

"From what you said, you made a quick decision!"

"I was under pressure from my agent. And I guess I didn't think it through."

"You didn't think it through, or you did, but you are still afraid of what you're feeling and decided this would be a good time to run away from it?"

Damn, Chris thought. *How does she read me like that?*

She knew him more than he knew himself and was quick to call him on his bullshit.

But what can I do about it? He needed her. That much he knew.

They were both so good for each other. But he was so afraid he would hurt her and tried everything not to, and here he was now, looking into eyes that were about to spill over with tears.

"Oh, Klara," he muttered, bringing her in for a hug. "I do commit to you. Fully. If you want to make this work long-distance, we can. I'm sure I can come back a few times during the year. It's not like it's forever."

Klara pushed him back and held him at arm's length, looking straight into his eyes. "Listen, Chris. I'm so happy for you. I really am. I know that offer is once in a lifetime. I don't blame you for taking it. I just wish you thought I was once in a lifetime, too. We clearly don't feel the same about each other."

Chris's mind raced. He was losing her, and he deserved to. She was right. She was once in a lifetime.

The book tour can wait, can't it? He started to panic and second-guess himself. Maybe he could figure out how to come back every month.

"Maybe I can figure out how—"

"No. Just go, Chris. I'm not letting you give up all you've worked hard for in life for me. Just go."

"But I—"

"No. I don't want to hear it. It's fine. You can come back one day and tell me all about your exploring."

"Okay, Klara. Is that what you want?"

Of course it's not what I want, you fool, she thought.

"It's what I want for you. I love you, and to love someone is to want them to be happy. I want you to be happy even if that means you're no longer in my life. I want what's best for you."

You're what's best for me, Chris thought.

But he had broken her enough. He knew he had to take the trip. All he could do was hope that they would cross paths again in the future, and maybe then he wouldn't be such a coward. But he also knew, by then, she would probably hope to never see his face again.

"Okay, Klara. I'll go. But I would've taken you with me. Know that. And I would've come back as much as possible for you. Know that, too. You make me feel ... like I've not felt ever before, and it does scare me."

Well, it doesn't scare you enough, Klara thought.

If Chris really were scared, he would be more scared of losing me, right? How can I expect him to give up his career for me anyway?

She realized she was acting a little like a spoiled brat. She wouldn't give up her career for him, and he wouldn't for her. He had a life. She had a life. They just happened to have a brief fling. Never mind that it was the most exciting and romantic thing to ever happen to Klara. It was just that—a brief fling. She should have stopped it that first time he left.

"We can keep in touch. I'm sure I'll hear your name around a lot anyway. Even if I don't want to," she said barely above a whisper.

"I will be sure to keep in touch with you. You've got a special place in my heart—always."

Klara just nodded and turned her attention back to the TV. Her heart completely shattered.

The kittens woke them early, swatting their noses until they got up to feed them. Klara wished she were used to this treatment by now, but she wasn't. She was a peon in her own house. The real asshole was Hazel, but they both were mischievous bastards. Twice in the last few days, she had awaken to something crashing in her living room. Usually, it was Hazel who had knocked something over. And she hadn't even accidentally done it, Klara was sure. Because, once, Klara had seen her sit next to a tiny ceramic-potted succulent, and the cat had just swiped her paw at it, knowingly knocking it to the ground. *Just for fun?* Klara had never seen any animal act like such a jerk before. Of course she'd had to adopt fur babies that were psychos. That was her luck.

"Shh … " Chris shushed the kittens. "You stay put, Klara. I'll feed them."

"No, I gotta get up anyway. Doesn't your flight leave early? I'll take you to the airport."

"I can get a cab. You go back to sleep."

"No way, Chris. I'm sending you off at least."

"Okay, okay. I'll make some coffee and feed the varmints."

Klara slowly lifted herself out of the bed and warmed her shower up. It was still dark outside, but a faint light was starting to come through her blinds. She wished she were back at the river, watching the sunset. Away from here and the good-bye she was about to swallow. She could feel her throat start to tighten as she held back tears. No use in crying now or again. She loved him and was letting him go. *That's what love is, right?*

The world tour was an amazing opportunity for his career. She couldn't fault him that. She just wished he hadn't cast her aside so easily. She thought he had loved her, but by now, if he did, he would have said it. He would have at least given her that because, truth be told, he had given her everything else.

Klara kept telling herself she was happy to have experienced the whirlwind romance she did. What was that heartbreaking quote? *Don't cry because it ended but smile because it happened.* Something like that. She tried. She would get through it. She always did.

She stepped out of the shower, drying herself with the brand-new fluffy towels she'd bought to impress him. He sat directly in front of her, on the bed and still undressed.

"I'm done in there. You can shower now," she said, keeping her eyes on his and not on his stupefying package.

"Come here." He pulled her toward him and onto his lap. His arms encircled her as he held her tight, passionately kissing her.

Klara pulled back, cupped his chin with her palms, and gently kissed his lips. "I can't do this. It's already hard enough. I just can't. Sorry, Chris."

"I understand. It's okay. I just wanted to remember us the way we were before all this," he said, waving his hands around at the drama surrounding them.

"I'm trying. I really am."

"I know you are," he said as he made his way to the shower.

Klara turned away from him, holding her breath and steadying herself. In just a few short hours, he would be gone. She could hold herself together until then at least. She slipped on her big-girl panties, put her hair up in a *this is business* bun, and prepared herself for the drive.

The airport wasn't very far from Klara's condo, so she made sure to drive extra, extra slow and prolong this last time she would see him. Her foot was barely on the gas pedal, and the radio was turned off. Silence. Complete silence was what she needed.

But Chris was the opposite. His nervousness made him chatty. He talked on and on about her book, her agent—who he knew as well—the publishing process, the kittens, her crack cookies, and every other detail from the weekend.

"Also, I'm going to send over my itinerary as soon as Marcy gets it to me, okay? You'll be able to track me anytime you want, or you know, come surprise me by waiting, naked, in my hotel bed. And also, don't let me forget; there's this app you'll have to download, so we can keep in touch with voice chats and texts. I'll get that to you, too. And, another thing, e-mail me when you hear from your agent. You have to let me know what's going on with your story. I'm so excited for you," he rambled on and on.

Klara only nodded back to him as they pulled into the parking lot. She was afraid to open her mouth or else she would let out a wail to wake the dead.

"Come on. I'll walk you in," she mumbled.

"You don't have to do that."

"I want to do that. Let's go send you off to your big adventure!" She smiled. Her voice strained and catching as she tried to fake her chipper mood.

Chris looked visibly uncomfortable but took her hand anyway and brought it to his lips. "You're the most amazing woman I've ever met, Klara Woods."

She winced and picked up his luggage. She was on the very edge of a really big ugly cry, and he had to go and keep being so damn dreamy.

They walked to the ticketing gate, hand in hand. Neither saying another word. Chris was agitated, biting his lip. Or was that to keep from crying? Klara didn't know what to think of his behavior, and she didn't have to anymore. No more guessing, no more hoping, just being. She struggled with the ever after.

Should I just forget about him like it never happened? Or should I be happy it did and hold on to the fond memories and embrace my heart being ripped to shreds? One day at a time. That's what I'll do. One day at a time, she thought.

"You'd better get in line. It looks like it might take a while." she nodded in the direction of security.

The line snaked around the lobby of the bustling airport.

"Okay."

"Okay."

Chris set his luggage down and went in for a full-on passionate embrace, jarring Klara from her weakness. She wanted to fight back, but she was already as limp as a dishrag, letting herself melt into him. She kissed him back with as much desire and ache as she could muster up in her very broken spirit.

They stayed like that, holding each other for what seemed like an eternity. But she was the first to let go.

"Thank you for everything, Chris. You've taught me so much in so little time. You've changed me. Completely. I feel like I know myself better, and I have a new outlook on life and where I want to go. I didn't have that before you. I just lived day to day, the same mundane routine. So, thank you for inspiring me to live a bit more," Klara muttered, gritting her teeth to hold back the tears.

He shook his head and took a deep breath. "It's you who changed me, Klara. Where once I lived in black and white, you've shown me color. You awakened me. If I could stay here … if I hadn't gotten the damn offer … I could … "

"No, let's not go down that road. Let's keep it bittersweet. No hard feelings. Okay?"

He nodded, and Klara could see his jaw was clenched, too.

"Remember not to be so tied down to your alarms, schedules, calendars. I see you blossom when you're free, Klara. My sweet, blossoming flower," he whispered as he leaned down and kissed her forehead. "Oh, and don't go falling into anyone again and hurting yourself for the sake of a fairy tale," he joked, trying to lighten the mood.

Some fairy tales are worth it, she thought as she curled into his chest and hugged him for what she knew would be the last time.

She could feel his heartbeat against hers. His hands tight on her back, pulling her into him. She took a deep breath, breathing him in one last time. Her head swimming with his scent. That was going to stick with her forever, she knew.

"Good-bye, Chris," she said, pulling away and turning to go before the floodgates were released and she looked like a fool. *Fools rush in, and this is what happens?* Her knees were beginning to feel like they were about to give out. She could feel the panic rise in her chest. She had to get out of there.

"Good-bye, Klara," he said, watching her quickly run in the opposite direction. The lump in his throat closing in as he bit his lip bloody.

He waited and waited to see if she would return, but eventually, he gave up and headed to his gate. She was gone, and she had taken a part of him with her.

Klara barely made it back to the car before tears started streaming down her face. She hopped in, locked the doors, and rested her head on the steering wheel as she gave herself up to grief. Her body shook with each sob. She couldn't drive back home now if she wanted to. She'd had her heart broken before, but this was on another level. She loved Chris with everything she had. He was her soul mate. At least, that was what she thought.

But do soul mates run away?

Her mind raced on how she was going to get through this, and she knew she would have to let him disappear. She took out her phone and blocked every single form of contact he had for her. Social media, gone. E-mail, gone. Phone, gone. It wasn't the first time she'd had to cut someone out of her life. It was just the way she dealt with things. Walls go up, and—*poof*—just like that, her heartbreaker disappeared. Klara knew it probably wasn't the healthiest way of dealing with life, but for now, it was her only choice to survive.

Chris looked out the window and down below as the plane took off. He could still smell her scent on his clothes, feel the grip of her hands clasped in his, her lips soft against his skin. He wondered if he would ever feel again the way he felt when he was with Klara. He closed his eyes and imagined her beside him, them both excitedly talking about their trip, seeing the world together. He imagined himself falling for her more and more. Letting himself go, letting himself love. Maybe even proposing to her overseas. Somewhere romantic. *A French café? A sunset in Rome? A chalet in Switzerland? If she had only said yes and thrown caution to the wind.* But he knew that wasn't Klara, and he knew it wasn't him either.

He put his head in his hands, taking deep breaths to steady himself.

"Fear of flying?" an older man said beside him.

"Huh? Oh, no. No, it's not the fear of flying that's got me today."

"I see." The man nodded. Unsure if he should press on.

Chris was visibly upset and looking desperate for help.

"I'm Scott," he offered his hand.

Chris was a bit embarrassed for anyone to see him as disheveled as he was, but maybe good conversation would get his mind off of the tragedy he'd just experienced.

"Nice to meet you, Scott. I'm Chris."

"Nice to meet you, too, Chris. I'm guessing you are either headed toward someone special or away from someone special. I don't mean to pry. You just look like you could use someone to talk to. I'm a pretty good listener. Scott Parker, psychologist, at your service. Aren't you in luck?"

"Good guess, but aren't we all running to or from something or someone special?"

"There are the select few who are content in not running at all. In just being. Some are at peace with themselves and living a solitary life; the others are psychopaths. No offense to you, but with your body language, I'm just trying to make sure I'm not sitting next to the latter."

"Ha! You're not. At least, I don't think I'm a psychopath. Are psychopaths self-aware anyway?"

"That's a whole other conversation. Deflection or stalling. Call it what you want. You don't have to talk to me about why your legs are shaking like you are trying to do the Watusi."

"The Wa what?"

"I'm showing my age, aren't I?" The man sighed.

Chris almost laughed. Almost. But even this silly old man would have a hard time breaking him out of his funk. *The Klara funk. Oh, she wouldn't like the sound of that*, he mused.

"I'm running away from someone special and toward something special," Chris began.

"So, you made a choice, is what you're saying," Scott prodded.

"Yes."

"And how do you feel about your decision?"

"Well, look at me. I'm a mess!"

Scott nodded in agreement. "We've got two hours on this flight. Let's sort it out."

"Really? I think it will take a lot longer than two hours to sort me out. I have these walls you see—"

"The walls, the walls. Everyone has the walls. You aren't the only one. Especially us men. We have fortresses. Not just walls. We're taught that we must be brave and not show emotion or else we will be weak! And, when we're weak, we get hurt. Or lose. Or both. Thankfully, in this day and age, the feminists are calling us out on this bullshit, and slowly, men are starting to feel safer about their emotions," Scott rambled on until he noticed Chris was staring at him in disbelief. "Sorry, I didn't mean to go off there on a tangent. It's just kind of my field, ya know? Would be easier on everyone involved if we just learned how to open up and be vulnerable. It's a risk but a risk that most of the time is worth taking. If not? Who cares? You live and learn."

Chris laughed at Scott's ramblings. "You sound just like her. She had told me the same things plenty of times."

"Okay, so it *is* a her. I got that out of you at least."

"Her name is Klara," Chris began.

It had been six weeks since she said good-bye to Chris. Six weeks of no contact, resulting in six weeks of French fries and ice cream, six weeks of crying into her pillow, six weeks of sappy romantic comedies on the TV, six weeks of too much wine on The Johnson farm, six weeks of taking Ms. May's banter without rebuttal. The first time she had seen Ms. May after he left, just the look on her face alone had told the old lady everything she needed to know.

"I'll kill him," she'd said, shaking her head, her hands on her hips.

All Klara could do was nod and fight back more tears.

Six weeks, she had been dead inside, all except for her writing. In those six weeks, she had written more than she had in the past six months. Which was a lot, considering her writing sessions with *him* had been very successful.

Her agent knew of her situation and joked that she should fall in love and out of love more often, maybe become a best seller.

Isn't that what all writers do? Write what we know?

Klara didn't feel like she knew much of anything these days. Her first book was launching in the spring, and that was what she turned her attention toward. The rest of the world was tuned out.

One day at a time, she thought each and every morning. *One day at a time ...*

Everyone told her that, one day, she would wake up, her head would be clear, and he would be out of it. For good. But she didn't believe it. No matter how much she tried to avoid thoughts of him, he was always there. She wondered often what he was up to in his travels and if he was upset at her for cutting him out. She wondered who he'd picked up as his new "travel guides" and what his next novel would be about. She wouldn't buy it, whatever it was. She couldn't bear to read dirty details in his stories, knowing where they were coming from—his muses. Not even if she was searching for herself in them. Nope, she wouldn't. She would just have Grayson pick it up and let her know. *That's not cheating, is it?*

Grayson and Klara had become closer since her breakup. She wouldn't be surprised if he was drawing hearts around their name with a BFF sign. Not only had he helped her ever since she showed up at their doorstep like a stray kitten, starving and nearly dead after her good-bye to *him*. But he'd also helped her with her writing. He was the perfect coach, the perfect test reader, the perfect slumber-party thrower, and the perfect partner in crime. Klara had even convinced Grayson to take up running with them in the morning, something that John had been trying to get him to do for months despite Grayson's protests of needing his beauty sleep.

Klara had begun calling Grayson Sleeping Beauty, and he loved every second of it. Sometimes, on the long runs or in a fit of laughter or with her hands in the dirt, cleaning up the beds before winter, she would forget about *him*. Or not exactly forget, but he wouldn't be front and center in her brain anymore. Just a warm memory in the back. Other times, he would be taking over her whole self, it seemed. She would catch the scent of his cologne in the air, hear a song they had sung together, see a sex scene on the TV that seemed familiar. All the moves that he used to pull on her. Damn, she missed the sex.

"Best way to get over someone is to get under someone else, Klara!" Grayson kept repeating each time he saw her.

But she wasn't ready for that. Besides, anyone after *him* would be a disappointment. A big letdown. Her body ached to feel his touch again. She missed that the most. That along with the dirty talk. The way the slight touch of his fingertips had sent a jolt of lightning down her spine and out her hoo-ha. Except he would describe it as his passion for her building up, dripping in anticipation, making her warm and wet between her thighs. Blushing pink, swollen, pulsing, waiting on him to fill her up.

Damn, he was so good, she thought.

Klara ached for that. But, instead of taking Grayson's advice and finding a lover, she channeled her unchecked libido into her writing. Her readers were either going to clutch their pearls or clutch their vibrators.

The days had turned into months faster than Klara realized. Her writing had taken off. She now had two novels accepted into the publishing world, and her third was well on the way. It turned out the best way to get over someone wasn't getting under someone but sticking her head in a computer and getting her emotions in print. She let that poor keyboard have it. Her fingers typing fast and furious as she recounted fights and slung them into her stories. Her fingers moving slow and sultry across the keyboard when she described the passion between her characters.

Everything she had been bottling up was spilling out and onto the screen. She only thought about Chris periodically now, like every other hour instead of by the minute. He was, after all, her muse. She couldn't fault him. Knowing him, he was probably still trying to call her, not getting the hint that she'd blocked him out of her life. *Not getting the hint or not accepting it? If he loved me, he would fight for me, right? And he didn't because he'd just left. Just freaking left.*

Klara could feel her temperature rising as she poured out her soul, her frustrations, her aches, her grievances, everything. And, when she looked up, months had already passed by.

The air was frigid. Holiday lights were beginning to be hung around town. Her world grew darker earlier, her days shorter. It was a perfect time to hibernate, which was what she normally would have planned to do. But, these days, she had been too busy. Her first book was due out next week, and her agent and Grayson had already put together the launch party. The Johnson used their connections and booked at a venue down by the river. A perfect place for the debut novel.

"You can see the bridge lights from there!" Grayson gushed.

Klara's voice caught in her throat as she remembered that one of those lights was hers. "That's … great! I know anything you put together will be fabulous. I can't wait to come!"

"To come? Darling, you *are* the party. This is about you. It's *your* party. You made it, Klara! Now, you get to relax, even if it's just for a night, and celebrate. Grayson-style," he said, dramatically flicking his scarf over his shoulder, turning, and walking away.

A break sounded foreign to Klara at the moment. Not that she wanted to take a break, but she hadn't had the need to just yet. Even with her last semester of classes, she was on a mission and unable to stop herself for once. Not when she was gaining success while forgetting about *him* anyway.

At least, she told herself she was forgetting about him. She'd had one night last week where her hands hovered over the keyboard as she hesitated to type his name into Google. Wondering what city he was in, what he was doing, how he was doing, who was he doing. But her better judgment, which was surprisingly improved these days, let her move on and continue writing instead of cyberstalking. She wished him well, wherever he was. She loved him enough to know that. She hoped he found his happiness, but she also hoped he remained single.

Because, let's be real, I'm not ready to let my mind go there yet.

She glanced at her calendar in front of her. Each day filled with work, school, and writing. Her weekends were spent writing as well, being at the farm or with her running group, or entertaining Ernestine and Hazel for the five minutes they were interested in her.

Ms. May was scheduled in here and there, too. She had been giving Klara lessons on baking, so she could "catch a man," but Klara knew it was just her way of saying she was trying to get Klara's mind off of that old, no good, rotten author douche bag who had torn her heart out and stomped on it. Even when Klara tried to explain that it wasn't really all his fault, Ms. May wouldn't hear it.

Klara surrounded herself with her friends, her kittens, and her writing to get her through the long winter months. With no time to think, she had no time to dream. Work, school, work, work, laughter, wine, school, work, work. That was all her brain understood these days, and that was all that mattered. One day at a time and one foot in front of the other would carry her into her future. But she knew he would always be in the back of her mind. She hoped his feet would carry him into his future as well. She only wished it had been a future with her in it, too.

FOURTEEN

Klara walked slowly through the bookstore. Her eyes wide as she read the signs and posters with her name in print. *Klara Woods*, Limerence *Book Signing, Today 10:00.* Still groggy from the launch party, she was handed a cup of coffee from her agent, Susan, and led to the back room. Her fingers reached out to touch the books as she made her way through the aisles.

Fiction. Nonfiction. True crime. Romance. She stopped at the display that held her novel. All hers. She had done it. Her heart and soul now tucked snugly between a front and back cover. Countless nights up revising, scraping it all together, and piecing it back again. Days spent writing proposals, researching, marketing, and importantly picking her emotions from her brain and displaying them for all the world to see. Klara had made it. *Finally.* At least, for now.

She checked her phone—no longer tied to alarms, but still a clock-watcher. It was almost time for her to begin. Her nerves left her hands slightly trembling. Her legs wobbled as if they could give out at any moment. How was she going to stand up in front of all these people and be picked apart? Her agent had advised her to read a passage from her book that was a little more scandalous, something provocative, but Klara wanted her audience to start at the beginning, her hook. Something that had a bit more meaning to her. She took a deep breath as she took in the curious faces around her. With knees slightly shaky, she walked up to the podium, introduced herself and her novel, and began reading an excerpt.

Emily's breath rattled throughout the halls. The flickering of the candles matching her raspy voice as it faded in and out. It was the middle of summer, but she was shivering with cold. Her teeth chattered as the chill creeped up her body and out of her breath.

"I can't breathe," she whispered.

"Hush," her husband said, calmly stroking her hair. "Look at me. Focus on me. Look into my eyes."

Her breath steadied as she held his gaze. Her lips inches away from his. His breath giving her life.

"John, I need you to know something."

"You don't."

"I do."

Emily's temperature rose, the fever encouraging her bravery or stupidity. She didn't know which, and she didn't care anymore.

John held her face, silently hoping she would fall asleep instead of making this harder for the both of them.

"Come on, Emily. You need some sleep. Close your eyes, dear."

"No!" she said, thrashing her head back and forth so as to shake her thoughts out clearly. Maybe the words would fall out of her mouth. Maybe she didn't have to say them. Maybe they would come on their own.

The nurse, hearing Emily wake, rushed to her side and called for the doctor. Emily coughed hard, her mouth filling with the metallic taste of blood. She could hear the doctor speaking as she drifted in and out of consciousness. If she didn't keep herself awake, her husband would never know, and her soul would never rest. Why was it so difficult to tell him?

They said your life flashed before your eyes as you lay, dying. But, for Emily, her regrets suddenly bubbled up, overtaking her thoughts. She saw no happiness. No laughing as she played with her sisters in the creek. No sitting beside the fire, watching her mother sew and mend their clothes. No Dad teaching her how to fish that first time summers ago. She didn't see John at their wedding or the way he'd looked at her when they first met. She didn't remember their first kiss or their first date.

Emily couldn't remember anything, except her regrets. That time she'd left her parents at sixteen, ashamed at where she had come from and determined to rise above it. The way her mom hung her head in sorrow as Emily had told her what an embarrassment she was. The way she'd left those kittens on the side of the road like her grandfather had told her to do when she was too young and too cowardly to stand up to him. And, worst of all, what she had done to John. All of her regrets haunted her in her feverish dreams. She needed to confess and apologize and right all of her wrongs. She had to; she could feel herself drifting away.

"I'm sorry, John. I—"

"Emily"—he took her hand—"whatever it is, it's okay. You're okay. You just need some sleep, and you'll be fine. We can talk about this later. You aren't yourself right now, honey. Please. Please get some rest. I'm not going anywhere. You can tell me all about it when you wake up."

"I don't want to wake up, John," she cried.

He stood up and slowly walked over to the window. He didn't want her to see his tears. He had been strong long enough for the both of them, and now that it was almost near the end, he could feel himself slipping. He turned back to look at her. She lay, glowing with sweat, pale and lifeless. The once-bright light of her eyes were now dimly lit and sputtering out. He knew she was right. She had been through enough and was ready to go. He couldn't blame her. He wasn't sure how she was still here, given all that she had been through these last few months. She was the strongest person he knew, and he wasn't able to let go.

"Please don't say that. I need you here. You're my everything, Em," he said, his voice quavering.

He didn't need her to say what she was going to say. He didn't want to know. He had heard rumors but ignored them. Not his Em, not her. She was the sweetest person he had ever known. Whatever it was she had to tell him, he couldn't stomach it. He knew it had to be bad for her to wait this long to come clean. Whatever it was she had done, speaking the words aloud, especially as it could be her last words, was not how he wanted to remember her.

"I know times are tough, Em, but you'll get through this. We'll get through this. You'll be outside in the sunshine by the end of the week. You just need some rest. That's all. Don't fret. Tell me your stories later."

He wiped his tears with the back of his hand and turned to tell her just how much he loved her. But he could already see her eyes frozen in a state of remorse, her lips parted and her chest still. Her secret caught in her throat, never to escape. She was gone. His body shook as he collapsed on the floor and cried with relief.

Klara looked out over the audience. She could tell who had already read the book and who hadn't. The nods of approval were her fans. The stricken glances came from those who hadn't yet decided to dive into *Limerence*. Maybe it wasn't the best passage to read aloud, but Klara was anything but conventional. She had done things mostly her way—mostly. And here she was now, in a bookstore, on a podium, reading her published work. It wasn't luck; it was sheer hard work and her infamous stubbornness.

The room was just a few rows deep, and not an empty chair was in sight. Most of her readers were women in their mid-forties, she noticed. But she did see a few men scattered about as well. Probably men who had been dragged here by their wives or men who would appreciate a good literary porn scene now and then because she definitely had those in her novel. It was titled *Limerence* after all. Not love, not smut, not erotica, just the feel-good emotions of limerence. Set in early eighteenth century and during the plague, of course. But still, limerence nonetheless.

Klara stood at the podium and continued explaining a bit about her book and her research into local history. Before her time was up, she asked for questions from the audience. She listened as the guests murmured to each other. A few asked more specific details about the history of certain places in her novel. Klara explained all she knew about the history, location, and life back then, as she knew it from research. She could see some of the audience members getting restless. She didn't blame them. They were asking the same questions over and over.

"Cut to the chase! We want to know how you wrote all that bumpin' and grindin', darlin'!"

Klara looked into the audience and straight into Ms. May's eyes. Of course it was Ms. May, and of course she would put Klara on the spot like that. She peered back at the old coot and laughed along with the audience. Her mind raced with the story she had prepared in case this came up.

"Honestly, I just read a lot of erotica to prepare myself," Klara said. Her eyes clouding over as she tried to hide the sadness she was surely displaying on her face.

She wanted to tell them it was *him*. She wanted to say his name aloud. She wanted to whisper it out and breathe it back in. She wanted to explain to them all how she'd had this person—*him*—come into her life and completely change the way she lived it. But she couldn't. She avoided any mention of him, any thoughts of him, and any late-night, drunken internet-stalking quests. It had been several months since their whirlwind rendezvous, and despite her having no contact with him, he still made a regular appearance in her brain. She was happy to remember, but as hard as she tried, she wished she could forget.

"Are ya sure, honey? I thought, as a writer, you supposed to write what you know. Aren't you single? You don't have some juicy tidbits for us?" Ms. May dragged on and on.

Klara held her breath. *Why is Ms. May doing this now? Couldn't she have asked me personally or waited until a more private time? Is she growing senile?*

Klara could feel her cheeks grow warm as the guests nodded in agreement. They looked to her, waiting for an answer.

"Writers do write what they know," a voice called from the back of the room.

Klara's heartbeat quickened as she met his gaze.

"This Farmer John character, does he have six-pack abs and like to run? I think I've seen him around town a time or two ... "

The room erupted in laughter as Chris and Ms. May looked across the room and nodded at each other in acknowledgment. If looks could kill, Chris would be dead. Ms. May looked just as alarmed as Klara. Behind Ms. May stood Grayson and the popular John himself. Grayson's hand was on his heart, and his jaw dropped as he slowly realized what was happening.

"Mmhmm. I rest my case," Ms. May muttered, holding her tongue for once so as not to cause a scene. She gripped her chair tight, restraining herself from walking over and popping Chris in the head.

The Johnson leaned in to whisper to Ms. May.

Klara glanced around the room, desperate for anyone to help her out. Her mind couldn't focus, and the room started to close in on her when she suddenly heard an alarm go off. The guests turned to Chris, scoffing at his phone's rude interruption.

"Sorry! Sorry!" he apologized loudly, giving Klara an out to excuse herself from the distracted audience.

"That's all right! My time is up now anyhow! But I will gladly answer your questions or sign your books at the front of the store. Thank you all so much for coming out!" Klara's knees trembled as she made her way to the front.

"I need fifteen minutes," she told her agent as she headed outside for some air. Her feet couldn't take her away fast enough.

What the hell is he doing here? she thought. Her mind was full of rage, but her eyes were on the verge of brimming over with tears. *How long has he been in town? How did he know about my book signing today? What in the hell was he thinking, just showing up, unannounced, and on such a big day as this?* The thoughts raced through her mind as she tried to rationalize it all and take it all in.

Klara kept her back to the doors as she stared out over the parking lot, thinking. She couldn't believe he was here. The second she'd heard that voice, she had known exactly who it was. The cold air hit her face, pushing her tears back up and into hiding. She sniffled, breathed deeply, and readied herself to face whatever was waiting for her back inside.

"Klara ... "

"No. Just ... no. You don't get to march back into my life. Not right now you don't. No, no, no, no," she said, turning to look at him.

His eyes looked frightened and ashamed, but also, she could feel it. That magnetic pull starting already between them both. His hands were fidgeting, ready to grab her and not let go. Hers were doing the same. Their legs unstable and weak.

"I'm not trying to ... I mean ... I want ... "

"Aren't you supposed to be off, touring the world and signing your own books? Now, I'm trying to sign mine, and I finally have a good thing going. You've been out of my head more often, and now, this. Now, you come back. For what? Do you want me to thank you for inspiration? Yes, thanks. You know that. Know what else I can thank you for? Leaving. Because you leaving is what led me to create this world for myself. So, thank you for coming into my life, leading me into believing in this happily ever after shit, and then peacing out. It's been brilliant writing material! Thank you, Chris!"

Klara turned to head back inside, leaving him outside and unsure of what to do with himself.

"Wait! We agreed, Klara," he said, shaking his head. "You told me to go. I thought that's what you wanted. I wanted you with me! You told me no! And, even after I left, I tried to keep up communication. You shut me out. I tried everything to get through to you. Believe me, I tried *everything*. I even came back a few weeks after we parted at the airport. I was here."

"You were what? You came here and didn't tell me? No stopping by to check in and see how I was doing?"

"You cut me out completely. Blocked me from everything. Do you really think you would have received me well? Or that I thought you would want to see me? I still came though. I needed you. I ached for you ... still do ... "

"But?"

"I was at the river," Chris sighed. "Remember the spot where we met? I was there, waiting for you. I woke up every morning at five a.m., so I could run into you and do the big, cheesy make-up kiss, and all the world would be right again. Except you weren't alone. I saw you with him, and you were happy and laughing."

"With who?"

"I don't know. Some man—tall, dark hair, underwear model— running alongside you."

She knew he meant Grayson. He was the only one who had been running with her aside from her group runs.

"That's my gay friend Grayson, you nimrod! It's Farmer John's lover!"

"What? So, you mean, you didn't pick up an underwear model after I left town?"

"No, I didn't pick up an underwear model! Good grief, Chris. Don't you know, I loved you? I told you that plenty of times before you left and ran from it. When you love someone, you don't just jump up and continue the life you lived before you fell in love. It takes a long damn time to heal."

"I know. I know that now."

She snorted, still skeptical and angry. Mostly at herself for shutting him out. What if she had known that he had come right back to her? Where would they be by now?

"So, you came back after we broke up? Why?" She could feel the tears welling up in her eyes.

"Yes, I came back. I know I should have told you I was coming, but I wanted this big, grand gesture that was actually, knowing what I know now, a very stupid idea. You just make me full of stupid. And all I want is for you to be happy, Klara. I wasn't going to ruin that. I would have preferred you happy with me, but I was the one who left. I should have fought harder, pushed harder, held on to you and not let go. Hell, I shouldn't have even considered leaving you in the first place," Chris said as he took a step toward her. "I didn't mean to cause all of this commotion. I just really wanted to see you again, hear your laugh one more time, and tell you how proud I am of you. Also, here, take this. I wanted to give this to you in person. It goes out next month. First copy, all yours." He handed her a large envelope.

Klara stood tall, still fighting back tears by remembering that trick she'd learned about in another one of those useless magazines. The article said to put your tongue to the roof of your mouth to avoid crying. The tears stayed back, but she was pretty sure the roof of her mouth would have a hickey by the time this conversation was up. She pulled out a manuscript from the envelope and thumbed through the pages. Her eyes darted back and forth between erotic passages that described her exact escapades with Chris. She kept flipping through the pages, finding bits and pieces of familiarity scattered throughout his latest romance novel.

He remained silent, watching her as she thumbed through the last few pages. She stopped and gave it back to him before finishing. He saw she had started to cry.

"I can't. Not now. I just can't." Klara tried to gather herself together.

She didn't want him to see her like this. She didn't want him to know that, after all this time, despite fighting it, the moment she had seen him again, she realized she was still, almost crazily, in love with him.

"How does it end, Chris?" she whispered, barely audible.

"He comes back."

"Yeah?"

"Yeah," he said as he stepped closer to her.

She stood up straight, her feet planted firmly on the ground. His face was inches from hers as they glared into each other's eyes. Their breathing becoming heavier and in sync. Klara's hands made fists as she physically tried to restrain her mind, her heart, her soul. She was losing again, but so was he. She could see it in his eyes. He was aching for her.

Damn it. I'm putty in his hands again and melting, she cursed herself.

"Why? Why did he come back?" she whispered into his mouth as her eyes naturally shut and the heat of him washed over her.

"Because he loves her," he whispered back before pulling her into him fully and kissing her.

The shouts and cheers coming from the store shocked Klara into remembering where she was and what she was doing. Behind her, the windows to the bookstore were full of people cheering and smiling. Her face reddened as she saw Ms. May nodding and winking at them both. The Johnson looked on. Grayson wiped his tears from his eyes. She even thought she saw a twinkle of a tear in John's eyes, too.

"I have to go. Do you want to meet later to talk about what just happened?"

"I'm not going anywhere. I've got to get in line and get a book signed! I heard there's a hot chick who writes borderline porn here!"

She laughed as she headed back indoors. Her agent grabbed her by the arm and steered her toward a table.

Ms. May called out to her as she passed by, "It's about damn time, honey. I was 'bout to go out there and kiss that boy myself!"

"I thought you said you wanted to kill him!" Klara shot back.

"Not when he talks like that I don't." Ms. May pulled at her collar, dramatically fanning herself. As usual.

"So, this title," he started, narrowing his eyes as they sat across from each other in their old meeting spot, the corner coffee shop.

Klara almost choked on her coffee. She thought about limerence and what all it meant to her. About how it had been something that royally pissed her off at first, but how it'd shaped her future in the end.

"Yeah, well ... ya see ... " she began, not knowing how to explain herself.

"I'm kidding. Now, I know it was a shit move on my part. It wasn't limerence, Klara. It was love. I was just too dumb to know that. I do now. And I'm so, so sorry."

"No, Chris, I'm sorry. I shouldn't have been a coward and cut you out of my life like that. You didn't deserve it. You had always been so good to me. I was just hurt and immature in dealing with it."

"I guess we both did some cowardly and immature things."

"I guess so. What made you decide to come back? How did you even do that? You are supposed to be overseas still."

"The first time I came back because I'd realized, you were my once-in-a-lifetime opportunity. You were right about that."

"I was what?"

"Right."

"No, say the whole sentence."

Chris rolled his eyes, knowing just how much she liked to hear that she was right. "Klara Woods was right. She was right, she was right, she was right! And I was wrong to doubt her."

"I didn't tell you that you were wrong, I just—"

"No, but I was. And that's why I came right back. As I was leaving, I actually met a man on the plane, who helped me out a lot. He talked sense into me."

"Oh, really? A stranger on the airplane convinced you to come back to me, but I couldn't? What did this old wise one say?"

"Basically that I was a dumbass." He shrugged. "That what I was feeling was love and I was too much of a chickenshit to admit it. That the feelings I had for you were special and that most people lived their whole lives not ever finding a person who made them feel like this. So, I decided to come back before I left for Europe. I wanted to try one last time. But, yeah, the old dude made me do it. Or didn't make me but convinced me of my own stupidity."

Klara laughed at that. She could only picture Chris's shocked face as this man called him out on his bullshit. She wished she could shake his hand or even hug the guy.

"I'm so sorry about that plan of yours. You waiting on me at the river and all. It does sound terribly romantic. I would have run to you, ya know. If I had known you were there, I would have run straight into your arms. If I had kept in touch with you and let you know about The Johnson—"

"Whose johnson? I thought you said he was gay!"

"No, no, no, silly." Her abs were starting to hurt from laughing.

They had only been together a few hours, and they'd immediately fallen back into the same old routine. She explained to him how she'd met The Johnson, all about Grayson and his newfound love of running. That was, until he got bored and moved on to something like goat yoga, which Klara had tried and wouldn't recommend unless you wanted poo pebbles surrounding you during savasana. Not the best way to relax. She rambled on and on about what her life had been like the last few months, and he, too, told her all about his travels.

Chris had been unable to write while he was overseas. His schedule had been so booked that he hardly even had time to research. And, when he finally did and got some time alone, his mind would wander. He was sure he saw the back of Klara as he passed by a café, or he would catch her scent in a department store in London. He would close his eyes at night, and there she would be, staring down at him, those beautiful curls he loved framing his face as she smiled. He missed those smiles. He missed the heat of her body. He missed the feel of her skin. He hadn't been happy over there. He'd had to come home, and Klara was home.

"So, you cut your trip short, is what you're saying?" she asked as he tried to explain his reason for coming back the second time.

"Yes. Canceled it. It's done and over. I'm here, and you're here. We're both in the same place, so … "

"For how long? When do you leave again?" Klara could feel her heart quicken. She could practically hear her pulse in her ears as she held her breath and waited.

"I don't have to leave. Unless you want me to."

"What do you mean? You're a Floridian. You live at the beach!"

"You can teach me how to be a Memphian? Besides, beach house is still there. It can be our winter home. Or, you know, we can split the time however you'd like. That is, if you're willing and if you want to give this a go … again."

She noticed his use of "our" home. *Is he really fully committing this time?*

"You won't go away again? You can stay here? What about your job?"

"The seminars are completely off the table until I get my writing back under control. But I figured we could talk about any opportunities coming up. If you want to go with me, you can. If you want me to stay, I will."

"I'll never stand in the way of your career, Chris."

"I know your stubborn ass won't. I'm not asking you to stand in the way but just to stand beside me."

"You know, if you break my heart again, Ms. May will cut you. You do know that, right?"

"I gathered that from the look she gave me back at the bookstore."

"Uh-huh. And Grayson will help bury your body."

"I'm sure he will. But I promise, never again. Let's break these walls down, both of us, and navigate this crazy love thing together."

"No more limerence?"

"There never was any."

EPILOGUE

The roaring Mississippi River churned on as the sun set over the horizon. It had been exactly two years since Chris saved Klara from her bad decision of bumping into a very much taken and very much gay Farmer John. Two years of ups. Two years of downs. Two years of growing. Together. Always together. The dark time overseas haunted Chris. It was a place he never wanted to return to. Not when he'd married the sunshine. Klara, too, tried to forget that low point in her life. She had been empty and incomplete. Now, she was happy *and* happily married.

They sat on the hill in complete silence, their hands intertwined as they took in the scene around them. The same spot they had met, the same spot they had married.

"Look around, darlin'. What do you see?" Chris said, turning toward Klara with a smile.

"Hmm ... well ... I see the sun setting over the river, the lights on the bridge starting to flicker on, the waves crashing into the shore, the tourists milling about. I see ... wait ... is she ..." Klara nodded toward a woman casually bending over to tie her shoe as she nervously looked up and around.

The woman stood right in line of a man barreling toward her, not paying attention to where he was going. His eyes instead on the sunset.

"Oh my gosh! It's you! Let's save her!" he said, hopping up.

"Wait! We shouldn't! Maybe that's her soul mate running toward her. Can't we just let fate happen?" she pleaded.

"It's not fate if we're here, watching a story we already know unfold! Now, come on," he replied, pulling her up.

"But we aren't exactly hot stuff for her to fall in love with! We're not a cute single man! It's different!"

"Maybe she is into threesomes?" Chris teased.

Klara elbowed him hard.

"Let me take this one over. Show you how it's done." She cracked her knuckles and bent her neck left and right as if to ready herself.

"All right, my little badass. You'd better hurry though. Someone's about to get hurt!"

She raced down the hill just in time to catch the runner, startling him as she touched his shoulder, making him stop. The woman stood feet before them, looking up, clearly frustrated with Klara.

Klara put her hands on her hips as the runner took his headphones out of his ears.

"You could have killed her! What are you doing out here, running full speed like that and not paying attention? You didn't see this woman in front of you, innocently tying her shoe? If I wasn't here, you would have stumbled right over and broken her gorgeous face! Look at her! I think you owe her an apology. She looks terrified," Klara dramatically spouted off.

The man looked terrified more than the woman, but that was what Klara wanted.

"I'm so sorry! I guess I wasn't—" the man started.

"You're damn right you weren't! You need to tell this lady you're sorry," she continued, turning toward the lady. "What's your name, miss?"

"Jenny," the woman answered, frightened. *Is this one of those crazy Memphians people talk about?* "I'm fine. Really, it's okay."

"No, it's not okay, Jenny! He could have killed you!" she said, turning back toward the runner. "I hope you can make it up to this poor, frightened woman in some way!" Klara muttered, turning around to leave and talking to herself like a maniac.

She could hear the couple nervously laughing behind her as she left the scene and walked back up to Chris, who stood in disbelief.

She gave him a high five, and they both sat back down in silence, watching the young couple now in conversation.

"Wow, that was much better than what I had done to you! You deserve a standing ovation for that one!" Chris laughed, putting his arm around Klara.

"Just setting them on the path toward limerence, is all. I've got a lot of experience in that area, ya see." She shrugged.

"Come here, you! I'll show you some limerence." Chris laughed as he pulled her toward him and into his arms.

"All the limerence I can handle?" she said, making her eyebrows dance on her forehead. She never quite got the hang of flirting.

"It's all yours, Mrs. Kaiser. All yours," he whispered in her ear, instantly making her melt. Again.

PLAYLIST

Curious as to what Klara was listening to on her morning runs? Check out these songs from the *Grit and Grind* playlist. If you'd like, you can listen to the whole playlist on Spotify. Search for Grit and Grind by Kat Addams.

"Crash Into Me" | Dave Matthews Band

"Stuttering (Kiss Me Again)" | Ben's Brother

"Memphis Sun" | Rival Sons

"Who's Your Farmer" | Chris Janson

"Stubborn Love" | The Lumineers

"All Shook Up" | Avila

"Big Jet Plane" | Angus & Julia Stone

"Oceans Away" | ARIZONA

"The Reason" | Hoobastank

ACKNOWLEDGMENTS

Writing has been a lifelong dream of mine, and I couldn't do it without the help of a good support system.

First and foremost, I want to thank my daughter. Without her, I wouldn't have the motivation to follow my dreams and show her that we can do anything if we believe in ourselves. My family has always backed me one hundred percent, and for that, I am incredibly grateful. A big thank-you to my dad for supporting me through my misadventures and loving me anyway. Even if he'll never know my true pen name because I'm an angel, and I totally don't write dirty stories!

I'd also like to thank the amazing sisterhood of support I've come to know in this indie author world. My awesome editor, Jovana Shirley, who held my hand several times when I had minor—or not-so-minor—freak-outs. My amazing cover designer, Lori Jackson, who not only is one of the most talented designers out there, but she also helped me above and beyond in introducing me to even more wonderful women in writing. Kelley Jefferson at Wonder PR, who offered me a wealth of information and guidance in every step of the way. And, to all of the hardworking authors that I've met who are also navigating this crazy writing world we so love, I am so grateful for you. I appreciate you. You're all rock stars. Let's do this.

To the Grind City—You stole my heart! I am beyond thrilled to be a part of such an amazing place and its amazing people. Memphis has some of the best and most relatable citizens. I see the work you all are doing to make Memphis better and better every day. Memphis, you rock! Grit and grind, baby! Grit and grind!

Last, but not least, I want to thank my friends who have been in my corner, cheering me on. The ones who have given me gold stars and more support, kindness, and inspiration than I ever thought possible. On days when I felt like climbing into a bed-fort instead of finishing this novel, my friends were always there to sing in my ear and encourage me to keep going. So, thank you. Five hundred and seven times over, thank you.

ABOUT THE AUTHOR

Kat Addams is a forever twenty-nine-year-old fashionista following her lifelong dream of writing contemporary romance inspired by the exotic men she meets in her worldly travels. At least, that's what she would like for you to think. She's certainly not a stay-at-home mom indulging in excessive daydreaming, frozen pizzas, an unhealthy addiction to purchasing pajamas, and one too many cocktails on the regular. That's some other romance author. The poor thing probably has to sneak away upstairs to write her dirty stories! What would her family think? Thankfully, that's not Kat!

Social Media:

Still crazy about Kat? Rawr! Stalk her on the social media platforms linked below! Also, please be sure to subscribe to Kat's newsletter for the latest news and a bonus free e-book (Check it out below!) You can find her newsletter on her website: www.kataddams.com/subscribe. By becoming a subscriber, you'll be the first to know the juicy details on upcoming releases. You'll also be the first to hear of special offers, exclusive content, sneak peeks, and more!

https://linktr.ee/author_kat_addams
(For all of the links in one convenient location!)

Newsletter: www.kataddams.com/subscribe
(Bonus *Hotty Toddy* Free E-Book)

www.goodreads.com/author/show/19253462.Kat_Addams

www.bookbub.com/profile/kat-addams

http://amazon.com/author/kataddams

Kat's Kittens: www.facebook.com/groups/651192492026240/
(A Facebook group to stay connected, laugh, and share.
Hope to see you there!)

www.facebook.com/KatAddamsAuthor

www.instagram.com/authorkataddams

https://twitter.com/KatAddamsAuthor

OTHER BOOKS BY KAT ADDAMS

COMING SOON!

Nashvegas Nights (Dirty South Series, Book 2)

Nashvegas Nights launches November 8, 2019, but is available now for preorder at https://amzn.to/31G38oY.
You can also add it to your Goodreads list at www.goodreads.com/author/show/19253462.Kat_Addams or Bookbub at www.bookbub.com/profile/kat-addams.

AVAILABLE NOW:

Hotty Toddy (A Dirty South Series Novella)

Exclusive & free to kataddams.com newsletter subscribers.

Jules Turner is all about peace, love, and light. She's always marched to the beat of her own drum, even when that beat took her far from her hometown of Oxford, Mississippi, and straight to sunny California. For the past ten years, she has been perfectly content to trade in her Southern roots for a yoga mat and herbal tea.

When her meddlesome mother suddenly interrupts Jules's namaste life by asking her to return for a visit, Jules knows her mom is probably scheming to play matchmaker ... again. She won't fall for it this time though ... except that she does—literally—landing right at the feet of her former flame.

Todd Miller—aka Hotty Toddy—is just as ruggedly gorgeous as he was in high school. When he learns that his teenage crush is back in town—and just in time for their ten-year reunion—he convinces Jules to come up with some scheming of their own. If Todd is lucky, their scheming will take them straight to the bedroom, where he tried—and failed—to seduce Jules on prom night so many years ago.

Pretending to be happily married, Todd and Jules strike out to fool their old high school bullies in the ultimate prank. But they quickly learn that they're really just fooling themselves. They can't just pretend. Not when they can't keep their hands off of each other.

How can two people who have been apart for so long connect again so quickly? What happens if their fake romance turns into something real? Will Todd be able to handle Jules's free-spirited adventures in California, or can he convince her to stay back in Mississippi and embrace her small-town roots?

With a little bit of scheming—okay, a lot of scheming—Jules just might find that her matchmaking mother knows best.